# Main Street

*Best Friends*

# Main Street

## *Best Friends*

# Ann M. Martin

SCHOLASTIC INC.

NEW YORK ◇ TORONTO ◇ LONDON ◇ AUCKLAND ◇ SYDNEY
MEXICO CITY ◇ NEW DELHI ◇ HONG KONG ◇ BUENOS AIRES

ISBN-13: 978-0-439-86882-2
ISBN-10: 0-439-86882-3

Illustrations by Dan Andreason

12 11 10 9 8 7 6 5 4 3 2 1          8 9 10 11 12 13/0

Printed in the U.S.A.                                    23

First printing, April 2008

*For Jane, sister extraordinaire*

# CHAPTER 1

# *Happy Birthday, Camden Falls!*

Whenever Flora Northrop looked back to that spring, she thought of it, rather dramatically, as the time of endings and beginnings. It was the spring in which she ended sixth grade, which was both her first and her last year at Camden Falls Elementary. It was the spring of graduations. It was the spring in which the Fongs had their baby. It was the spring in which two Camden Falls citizens got their very first jobs. It was the spring in which the town celebrated its 350th birthday, ending more than a year of preparation and anticipation. And it was the spring in which Flora and her sister, Ruby, ended their first year in Camden Falls and began the next one.

Flora's first winter in her new home had been long, cold, and very snowy. Flora had enjoyed it (school had been closed six times since December — four times for snow and twice for ice), but on a late March day when warm breezes brought signs of spring, she breathed in deeply and found herself thinking of blooming flowers and buzzing bees and Popsicles from the ice-cream truck. Unfortunately, she was so busy thinking of these things that she didn't realize that Mr. Donaldson, her teacher, was looking her way. He'd been saying something, but she wasn't sure what, and now he was waiting for some kind of response from her.

"Um," Flora said, drawing her breath in sharply. This was a very un-Flora-like moment, and she could feel herself blush.

The good thing about Mr. Donaldson, which had made him a popular teacher in the few months since he had taken over Flora's class, was that instead of becoming impatient with her, he said, "It's hard to concentrate on a day like today, isn't it?"

Flora let out her breath. "Yes," she agreed. Her eyes strayed to the windows again and then to the door near Mr. Donaldson's desk, the one that led to the courtyard. Mr. Donaldson had opened it wide, and Flora knew she wasn't the only student in her class whose thoughts were on flowers and bees and Popsicles.

"That gives me an idea," said Mr. Donaldson, glancing at the clock. "Tonight's homework is a composition. I was going to ask you to write about pets, real or imaginary, but why don't you write about summer vacation instead. Today is a good day for thinking about that. It isn't really so far off."

When class ended, Flora leaped from her seat, eager to catch up with her friends Olivia and Nikki. On her way to the door, she paused by Mr. Donaldson's desk and whispered to him, "I'm sorry I wasn't paying attention."

"No problem," he replied. "I suspect you were daydreaming about the weather. Weather will be good material for your composition."

In the hallway, Flora linked arms with Olivia and Nikki and said, "Ruby has a play rehearsal now. Let's watch for a few minutes before we go home. You're coming with us today, right, Nikki?"

Nikki nodded. "Yup. I'm not taking the bus. Tobias is going to pick me up at Needle and Thread later."

Arm in arm, Flora and her friends hustled through the halls toward the auditorium, and Flora thought, as she had many times in the months since school began, how very lucky she was to have two friends as wonderful as Olivia Walter and Nikki Sherman. She and Olivia and Nikki were not popular kids. Not by a long shot. But they weren't unpopular, either. They were just themselves — and lucky to have found one another.

Olivia was small for her age and had skipped a grade to boot, making her the youngest and tiniest kid in the entire sixth grade. She was also the smartest, brimming with enthusiasm for everything school offered, especially science. Sometimes Flora found it hard to muster excitement over fishers (mammals that apparently had nothing to do with fishing) or milkweed pods or monarch butterflies. But she tried for her friend's sake.

Nikki, whose mother struggled to hold the Shermans together, lived in a lonely and run-down house in the country. She often showed up at school wearing clothes that were faded and baggy, having previously belonged to Tobias, her brother, who was so much older than Nikki that he could drive. Her classmates paid little attention to her other than to poke her occasionally in the hallway or stick a nasty, anonymous note (usually full of misspellings, which Nikki pointed out to Olivia and Flora) in her locker.

Flora was shy — so shy she dreaded being called on or asked to read in front of the class or (worst of all) having to stand before the class to make a speech. She would blush to the very roots of her hair. Furthermore, Flora had become an orphan, an actual orphan, the year before, and her classmates did not know what to make of this. So mostly they left Flora to herself, which meant that Flora and Olivia and Nikki had formed a small but impenetrable group.

Ruby Northrop, fourth-grade celebrity, was part of this group, too, but she was nothing like the others. She was not a particularly good or enthusiastic student, she had a flair for style, she was far from shy, and she had made many friends since moving to Camden Falls. She sang, she danced, and she had been tapped to perform in the school play, which was to be an important part of the upcoming town birthday celebration.

Flora, Olivia, and Nikki came to a halt outside the door to the auditorium. Olivia opened it silently and the girls slipped inside.

"There she is," whispered Flora, pointing to her sister, who was sitting in the first row of seats. Flora studied the kids on the stage. "This isn't one of Ruby's scenes," she added.

The play, *The Witches of Camden Falls*, was based on an unfortunate period in the history of Camden Falls, during which ordinary (and very unlucky) citizens, thought to be witches, had been persecuted and punished. Ruby was the star of the play.

"Then let's go," said Olivia. "I don't want to hang around unless we can watch Ruby."

So as silently as they had entered the auditorium, the girls left it and then left their school.

"Ahh!" said Nikki, breathing in deeply as they turned onto Aiken Avenue. "Spring."

"What a great spring this is going to be," said Flora. "The Fongs will have their baby." (The Fongs lived at one end of the Row Houses, in which Flora, Ruby, and Olivia also lived. Flora was making a dress for their baby.)

"My parents will open our store," said Olivia.

"Really? So soon?" said Nikki.

"Yup," said Olivia, who didn't think it sounded soon at all. Her father had lost his job way back the summer before, and it had taken months for him and Olivia's mother to decide what they were going to do next.

"We'll finally have the big celebration," said Nikki as they passed a sign reading HAPPY BIRTHDAY, CAMDEN FALLS! JOIN US MAY 24TH–26TH FOR THE BIGGEST BIRTHDAY PARTY EVER! PARADE, CARNIVAL, FIREWORKS, CONTESTS.

"You know what else is going to happen this spring?" asked Flora.

"Yes," Olivia replied glumly. "We'll graduate from Camden Falls Elementary."

"Don't you *want* to graduate?" asked Nikki.

"Well, I don't want to flunk out," said Olivia, "which would be impossible anyway. But I don't want to leave, either. It's the only school I've ever gone to, except for preschool. I've been at CFE since kindergarten. This is my seventh year there."

"Mine, too," said Nikki.

"Seven years of walking to school," Olivia went on dreamily. "Seven years along this same route. Day after day after day." She turned her face to the sun. "I wonder how many walks that is. Let's see. Seven times . . . how many school days are there in a year? I need my calculator." She looked at Nikki. "Don't you mind that we'll be leaving?"

"I don't know. I'm kind of excited about the central school," Nikki replied. "Even though Tobias will graduate in June, so we won't get to be there together."

"Ahem," said Flora. "I wasn't talking about graduation."

"What?" said Nikki and Olivia, looking puzzled.

"I asked you guys about what else is going to happen because I wanted to tell you that I found out last night my friend Annika is coming for a visit."

"Annika Lindgren from your old town?" said Olivia. "Coming here?"

Flora nodded. "She and her parents want to come for the weekend of the birthday celebration. That is going to be so cool. I haven't seen Annika since last June, since the day Ruby and I moved here with Min."

Nikki started to speak, hesitated, then finally said, "Was it Annika's mother who came to the hospital to get you and Ruby after, you know . . . ?"

"It's funny, but I've never been able to remember who came that night," Flora replied slowly. "It was either Mrs. Lindgren or Min. I remember giving the police officer both of their phone numbers. Mrs. Lindgren must have come since she was so much closer."

It was on that January night — the night of the hospital and the police and the phone calls — that

Flora and Ruby had become orphans. An accident on a snowy road had taken the lives of their parents and changed Flora's and Ruby's lives in ways they couldn't have imagined. Min, their grandmother, had traveled from Camden Falls (along with Daisy Dear, her beloved golden retriever) to the town in which Flora and Ruby had grown up and had stayed with them until things settled down. In June, when the school year ended, she had packed up their belongings and moved them back to Camden Falls, into the house in which both Min and the girls' own mother had themselves grown up. The last year (*more* than a year now since the accident, Flora reminded herself with mild surprise) had been difficult and sad. It had also been a year in which Flora and Ruby had made new friends — not only Olivia and Nikki but all their neighbors at the Row Houses (just for starters). And a busy year full of school and projects and classes and events.

Really, Flora thought, if she had to leave her home and start a new life, she couldn't be much luckier than to move in with a grandmother who co-owned a sewing store (the other owner was Olivia's grandmother Gigi). Flora's passion was needlework and crafts, and now she spent frequent afternoons at Needle and Thread, working on projects that Min and Gigi displayed in the window, learning new techniques, and sometimes even helping to teach classes.

"So Annika will be here for the whole weekend?"

Olivia asked, and Flora reeled her mind back to her friends and their conversation.

"Yup. The whole weekend."

There was a short silence and then Olivia said, "Annika was your best friend, right?"

Flora nodded. "We met in first grade. We were always having sleepovers and —"

"Did she live next door to you?"

"No. She lived a few streets away."

"But she was your best friend?" said Olivia again.

Flora glanced at her. "Yes. Just like you and Nikki are my best friends now."

"Cool," said Nikki.

Nikki was about to ask Flora if she missed her old town when Flora said, "Hey, Olivia, let's go to your store before we go to Needle and Thread."

Olivia grinned. "My store. That sounds so, I don't know, *important*."

"It is!" said Flora. "And it's really exciting."

The girls turned right onto Dodds Lane and then right again, this time onto Main Street. They walked along the west side of the street, passing Needle and Thread (Flora and Olivia waved to their grandmothers through the window), then Zack's hardware store and Heaven, the jewelry store, before reaching the old building that was slowly being transformed into Sincerely Yours. The girls peeked inside. The kitchen in Sincerely Yours was being renovated so it could be better used to prepare Mrs. Walter's specialties — jams and baked goods and candies of all kinds — and in the front of the store a counter was being installed at which the food would be sold, and shelves were being built to hold all the items that could go into the custom-made gift baskets the store would also sell.

"I see Mom inside talking to the contractor," said Olivia, nose to the glass. "I think Dad's at home waiting for Henry and Jack to come back from school. We'd better not bother Mom now. Let's go see Min and Gigi."

Flora, Nikki, and Olivia ambled back to Needle and Thread. When Flora opened the door and stepped inside, breathing in the particular smells of the store, it seemed that she was walking into the heart of her world. Her home at the Row Houses was special, that was true, but Needle and Thread sometimes felt like the center of everything. Here was where she and Min and Gigi were helping with the costumes for Ruby's play. Here was where they were working on the Needle and Thread float for the parade in May. Here was where Flora had gotten the idea for the dress she was making for the Fongs' baby. And here was where the important people in Flora's new life often congregated.

Just now, for instance, she found not only Min and Gigi but Mr. Pennington and his dog, Jacques, who had stopped in for a visit; Sonny Sutphin in his wheelchair, also visiting; and Mary Woolsey, working away at her sewing machine in the back of the store. Flora felt like shouting, "I'm here, everybody!" as Ruby might have done, but instead she just smiled, happy to find so many of her favorite people close at hand.

She called hello to Min and Gigi, and they waved back, Min in a hurry, which made Flora smile. "Min" was short not just for Mindy but for "in a minute," since she was such a busy person.

Flora sat on the couch and patted Jacques, while Mr. Pennington, who lived next to Olivia at the Row Houses, said, "The first true day of spring!" and then told Flora that he planned to plant his vegetable garden soon.

Flora greeted Sonny, who was on his way out of the store, and he replied, "Happy news, Flora. I've decided to look for a job." For as long as most people in Camden Falls could remember, Sonny had spent his days roaming town in his wheelchair, a cheerful presence, a fixture on Main Street, but somehow unconnected to his very own world.

Next, Flora spoke to Mary (known to many of the local children as Scary Mary but now Flora's friend), who said, "I had a good idea for your research project. It occurred to me that you should get in touch with Mrs. Jacob Fitzpatrick. She's one of my sewing customers and she's lived here all her life. She'll have some interesting stories about the Great Depression."

"Thank you," said Flora.

And then she thought about the changes that were looming — graduation and the new baby and the opening of Olivia's store and Sonny's job and what she might learn from Mrs. Jacob Fitzpatrick — and she felt as she did when she stood on the beach, the ocean sweeping away from her, and put her foot out to stick one toe in the chilly water.

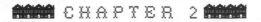

# CHAPTER 2

# In the Country

Min and Gigi were closing Needle and Thread for the day when Tobias Sherman cruised down Main Street and pulled up in front of the store.

"There's Tobias!" Nikki called. "I have to go!"

"Bye! See you tomorrow," said Olivia and Flora.

Nikki hesitated just briefly before climbing into Tobias's car. The car, like many things in Nikki's life, was run-down and shabby. Tobias had once complained to his mother that the kids at school teased him about the condition of the car, and Mrs. Sherman had replied, "Then tell them it's a work in progress."

This was true. Tobias was frequently painting it, tuning it up, tinkering with it. Nikki herself didn't care *too* much what the car looked like as long as it ran. And the fact that it ran at all was due to Tobias, who had taken a wreck and made the engine purr like a kitten.

"Hi!" said Nikki as she fastened her seat belt.

"Greetings," Tobias replied, and Nikki giggled. Then she looked at the clock on the dashboard. "Just in time to pick up Mae," she said. Mae's afternoon day care center closed at five-thirty, and Tobias and Nikki, who sometimes picked up their little sister at the end of the day, knew better than to be late.

"What time is Mom coming home tonight?" asked Nikki.

"Let's see. This is Wednesday? She works at both places today, so six-thirty."

Nikki was silent.

"What's wrong?" asked Tobias.

Nikki scowled. "Did Dad *ever* send us a *single* penny?"

"Nope. And let's not get off on that subject again. It's just going to make both of us mad. Look. Here's Happy Days." Tobias rolled his eyes. "What a lame name for a day care center. Couldn't they come up with anything better?"

"Even Mae thinks it's silly," Nikki agreed.

"There she is." Tobias pointed to the playground, where their six-year-old sister was hanging upside down from the monkey bars, her open jacket falling from her shoulders.

"Mae!" Nikki called, climbing out of the car. Then, "Hi, Mrs. Mines!"

"Hi, Nikki," replied the teacher on playground duty. "Your mother called this morning and said you and Tobias would be picking up Mae today. She's all ready to go. There's her backpack."

"Nikki! Nikki!" cried Mae then, righting herself before throwing her arms around her big sister.

Later, as Tobias drove them along the country roads outside of Camden Falls, Mae reported cheerfully from her spot in the backseat, "In school we learned about fish today, and then at day care we learned a song about fish. I don't know if I remember all the words, but here, listen: *Down in the meadow in an itty-bitty poo fam fee itty fitties and their mama fitty, too. "Fim!" said the mama fitty. "Fim if you can —""*

"Excuse me, what?" said Tobias.

"I'm not sure what it means, either," Mae admitted, "but our teacher said it's about fish, and it's really fun to sing. Later you get to say, *'Boop, boop, dittum, dattum, wattum, CHOO!'* a lot of times."

Tobias turned off the road and onto the lane that led to the Shermans' house. Nikki opened her window. "Ahh," she said. "Smells good. Flora got caught daydreaming in school this afternoon because our door was open and it was practically summer out."

"It's summer?" said Mae.

"Not really. It's still early spring," Nikki replied. "But it smells like summer today."

"Can we walk to the Shaws' farm?" asked Mae.

"Maybe this weekend," said Tobias.

Nikki breathed in the smells of damp earth and new green shoots, of things growing and changing and emerging. She wished her yard looked like Flora and Ruby's or Olivia's, wished it looked like most of the yards in town. She imagined green lawns and flower beds and rambling rock walls. She imagined wide front porches, some with swings. She looked at her house. The wooden steps had recently grown crooked. The paint was peeling faster than ever. And the yard — well, there wasn't really a yard at all. Just packed earth and small ramshackle buildings and the burning pit. Nikki sighed.

Her father had left home four months earlier, soon after Thanksgiving, supposedly to take a job somewhere in the South. He left with grudging promises to write and send money. Neither letters nor cash had arrived, although Mr. Sherman himself had returned briefly at Christmastime. He'd stayed just long enough to horrify and frighten all the Shermans, and then Tobias, enraged, had thrown his father out of the house.

"He won't come back now," Mrs. Sherman had said that night. "He's humiliated."

Nikki hoped that was true — but with her father, you never knew.

Tobias parked the car and Nikki stepped out, then helped Mae with her backpack.

"This weighs a ton," she said. "What's in here? Rocks?"

"No," said Mae, giggling. "We cleaned out our desks."

Nikki peeked in the backpack. "You had sneakers in your desk? And . . . where did all these books come from?"

"From my teacher," Mae replied. "She let me borrow them. I have to — hey, Nikki! Tobias! Look!"

Nikki turned her head in the direction Mae was pointing. At the edge of the property, where the shrubs and bushes formed a sloppy divider between their yard and the south side of the Shaws' land, sat two skinny dogs.

Nikki considered them. "Well . . ." she said.

"Can we feed them?" asked Mae. "Can we keep them?"

"We definitely can't keep them," said Tobias.

"But we can feed them until the people from Sheltering Arms come out here again," said Nikki.

Stray dogs were always showing up in the Shermans' yard. Nikki supposed they roamed the countryside, dogs that were lost or abandoned or feral. She and Mae used to feed them, but eventually so many came by for meals that Nikki could no longer afford their food. Finally, Tobias had taken her to the animal shelter, and the people there had started coming by to trap the stray dogs (humanely) and find homes for them.

"Maybe we could keep just one of them," said Mae, turning hopeful eyes to her brother and sister.

"Nope. Can't afford it," said Tobias.

"Besides, what would Paw-Paw think?" asked Nikki.

"That he had a new friend?" said Mae, but she didn't press the point. She ran ahead of Tobias and Nikki and threw her arms around Paw-Paw, the Shermans' only pet, who himself had once been one of the stray dogs.

By the time Mrs. Sherman returned from work, Tobias had started supper and Nikki had started her homework, having first listened to Mae do her fifteen minutes of reading aloud.

"I'm exhausted!" exclaimed Mrs. Sherman, tossing her coat and handbag on the couch, then flopping onto a chair at the kitchen table.

Nikki regarded her mother seriously. "How long do you think you can keep this up?"

"Keep what up?"

"Two jobs."

"I don't know."

For two months now, Mrs. Sherman had been working both as a cashier at the new grocery store in Camden Falls and as a waitress at Fig Tree, the fancy restaurant on Main Street. Tobias worked, too, after school and on weekends. The Shermans were getting by, but just barely.

"I'm trying to find a new job," said Mrs. Sherman, and by this she meant a full-time job with better pay and better hours, "but it's hard to job hunt when I'm working."

"Well," said Tobias, who by now had called Mae to the table and filled everyone's plates, "when school ends and I graduate, I can help by getting a full-time job."

Nikki eyed her mother and wasn't surprised when Mrs. Sherman said, "That's very nice, honey. I really appreciate the thought. We all do. But you have your own life to live. I don't want you to feel you have to help support us. Not after you graduate. Speaking of which, what about college?"

Tobias looked up with his mouth full. "What?"

"College," his mother repeated. "I know we should have been thinking about this, um, years ago, actually, but there were always so many other . . ." Her voice trailed off.

"It's okay, Mom," said Tobias.

"No, it isn't. And now that I'm in charge around here" (Mrs. Sherman glanced at Mr. Sherman's empty chair), "I intend to do things differently. I have different goals for you kids. I always have." She paused. "Anyway, you graduate in June, and then wouldn't you like to go to college?"

"How would that be possible?" asked Tobias. "We can't afford it. I haven't even applied anywhere."

Mrs. Sherman put her fork down. "There are ways to do everything."

"You wanted to go to college, didn't you, Mom?" asked Nikki, who very much wanted to go to college herself one day.

"Yes. And I've always regretted not going."

"Maybe you could go to college now," said Tobias, inspired. "Really, Mom. You always read stories about old people — I mean, people your age — who go back to school and get their college degrees."

"Let's concentrate on you first," said his mother.

After the dishes had been washed and dried, Tobias went outside to one of the sheds in which he tinkered with complicated mechanical and electrical things that mystified Nikki, while Mrs. Sherman and Mae emptied Mae's backpack and looked through the books her teacher had lent her. This gave Nikki the bedroom, the one she shared with her sister, all to herself for a solid hour. She sat at the scarred desk (bought three years ago at a garage sale) with Paw-Paw at her feet.

Nikki, one of the best students in Mr. Donaldson's class, pulled out her battered notebook. She had every intention of writing the essay about summer before doing anything else, but when she opened her drawer to look for a pencil, her eyes fell on a sheaf of papers, and she pulled them out and smoothed them flat. Here were some of Nikki's drawings from the previous summer — a sketch of a dragonfly, which now struck her as embarrassingly amateurish, but also a more finished drawing of a grasshopper, which she thought was quite good. Nikki planned to enter some of her best drawings in the art exhibit that was to be a part of the Camden Falls birthday festivities. She threw away the dragonfly sketch but decided to add the grasshopper to her exhibit folder.

The exhibit folder sat on top of the desk, right out in the open. Nikki still marveled at this. Her father had frowned on her interest in art. In fact, he had not had very nice things to say about artists or about art as a profession. At the beginning of the school year, before Mr. Sherman had left, Nikki was still drawing in secret and had been able only to dream about the exhibit. Now she could draw whenever she felt the urge, and she could leave her work lying around the house without worrying about what her father might do to it. She had told Mr. Donaldson that she planned to enter three finished pieces in the exhibit in May. Still, sometimes when Nikki looked through the folder, a small part of her worried that her mother had been wrong; that maybe her father hadn't been humiliated enough to leave for good. What if he came back again unexpectedly — for Mae's birthday or Tobias's high school graduation or for no reason at all?

Nikki considered hiding the folder, but the fact that thinking of her father made her want to do this angered her. She left the folder where it was and began her composition for Mr. Donaldson.

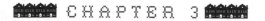 

# CHAPTER 3

# Sincerely Yours

There was nothing, Olivia thought, like stepping through her front door and seeing the yards of the Row Houses spreading away in either direction up and down Aiken Avenue. The sight was especially good on a bright morning in the early spring. To her left were the yards belonging to the Fongs and the Edwardses and Mr. Pennington. The Fongs' yard had recently been transformed from the traditional flower beds and grass to islands of stones, a reflecting pool, and some empty gardens that Mrs. Fong had told Olivia would soon be filled with nonflowering greens. Did Olivia know what ornamental grasses were? Olivia didn't, but she liked the Fongs' new look very much, so she thought she would like ornamental grasses as well.

The Fongs' yard was empty of people on this early morning, as was the Edwardses', but Mr. Pennington was sweeping his walk while Jacques dozed in the sun on the front stoop. Farther along, to Olivia's right, old Mr. Willet was climbing into his car, and Olivia thought perhaps he was on his way to visit Mrs. Willet, who had Alzheimer's and had recently moved to a nursing facility. At the far end of the row, the four Morris children were taking advantage of this unusually warm March Saturday to play noisily and vigorously in the grass, which was just beginning to lose its winter brown.

Olivia now leaned back into her house and called, "Henry! Jack! Come on! I want to go. Flora and Ruby are waiting for me."

Presently, Olivia's brothers, ages eight and six, thundered down the stairs and out the door. "All right," said Olivia. "Now remember: Mom and Dad are going to be at the store all morning, so you're going to stay with the Morrises. I'm going into town with Flora and Ruby."

"Okay!" said Jack.

"Bye!" said Henry.

They ran across the lawns to the Morris kids, while at Min's house, Flora fumbled for her key and Ruby called admonitions to Daisy Dear and King Comma, their cat, who, Olivia presumed, were standing on the other side of the front door.

"No fighting while we're gone," Ruby said. "Daisy, you're in charge. King, no clawing the furniture."

Olivia ran to her friends and soon they were walking toward Main Street.

"Do you think," said Ruby, "that after Sincerely Yours opens you'll get free candy anytime you want it?"

Olivia wrinkled her nose. "I don't know. Anyway, I'm a little tired of candy. I like it, but Mom's been making it at home for so long that it's not exactly special anymore."

Ruby sighed. "It would be for me. I wish I lived in Candyland."

Olivia and Flora and Ruby passed Needle and Thread, waving vaguely toward the windows as they did so. A moment later, Flora exclaimed, "Hey, the sign is up!"

Sure enough, a long white sign with staid black letters spelling out SINCERELY YOURS had appeared over the door to the Walters' store.

"Sweet," said Ruby.

"It looks busy inside," commented Flora.

Olivia opened the door. The store was still a mess, but perhaps not as messy as it had been a few weeks earlier. Plywood was stacked here and there, with paint cans, rags, rollers, toolboxes, sawhorses, ladders, and drop cloths arranged tidily along the walls.

Olivia's parents were smiling.

"What do you think, girls?" Mr. Walter asked Flora and Ruby.

"It's going to be beautiful," said Flora politely.

"Where will the candy be?" asked Ruby, and Flora gave her a tiny pinch. When Ruby had an idea in her head, it was hard to get it out.

"We'll be making it in the kitchen," replied Mrs. Walter. "The kitchen is in the back, through that doorway. And we'll be selling it here at the counter. The counter should be completed in about three weeks."

"Guess what," said Mr. Walter. "We think we might be able to have the grand opening just before the three hundred and fiftieth birthday party."

"Really?" exclaimed Olivia. "Excellent!"

"What will you do for the grand opening?" asked Flora.

"We're not sure yet," said Mrs. Walter. "Some kind of party."

"With free candy?" asked Ruby.

"Ruby!" said Flora in a loud whisper. "Stop!"

"It's a fair question," said Ruby.

"Yes, I believe there will be free candy," said Mr. Walter.

The door to Sincerely Yours stood open on this warm day, and several people who were passing paused to peek inside. Then a voice called, "Hello, neighbors!" and Sheila from Heaven entered the store.

"I guess we *are* your neighbors, aren't we?" said Mrs. Walter.

Min was the next to stop in. "It's really coming along," she said approvingly, surveying the space.

Three more visitors arrived, and Olivia heard Robby Edwards call cheerfully, "Hello! Hello, everyone! Hi, Olivia! Hi, Flora! Hi, Ruby! Hi —"

Mrs. Edwards took her son by the elbow and said gently, "I know this is exciting, Robby, but try to calm down."

"But it's a new store, Mom! Olivia's store! A candy store! And more!"

"Robby."

"Okay." Robby Edwards, eighteen years old, stepped back through the door and stood outside for a few moments, breathing deeply. Olivia watched him through a clean spot on the window. Robby had Down syndrome and sometimes became overexcited. Now he entered the store again and whispered to Olivia, "It's time for appropriate behavior."

Mr. Walter was showing Mr. Edwards around the store. "We had to start all over with an entirely new kitchen," he explained.

Robby waited patiently until Mr. Walter had finished the tour. Then he said, "Mr. and Mrs. Walter, I have to ask you a question. May I please apply for a job here? I graduate in June. Then I'm going to go to work. We've talked about it," he added, glancing at his parents. "This is a serious decision."

"It is indeed," Mrs. Walter started to reply, but she was interrupted by Mrs. Edwards.

"We talked about your finding a job," said Robby's mother, "but not about applying for work *here*. You didn't discuss that with us."

"But I'm an adult now," said Robby. "I have to start doing things on my own."

Olivia looked at Mrs. Edwards, who was watching Robby with a mixture of fondness and sadness. "Robby, this is not the place for such a discussion," she said gently.

"Excuse me," was Robby's reply. "Mrs. Walter, I've been learning about making change and stocking shelves and being polite to the customers and not shouting at people or crying if they say something I don't like. Oh, and using my quiet voice. And I'm good at memorizing things. And also I can use a calculator."

"That's very impressive," said Mr. Walter, who had joined Olivia's mother. "The thing is, we haven't thought much about who we're going to hire."

"We were concentrating on finishing the renovations and planning the opening," added Mrs. Walter.

"But it's good to think ahead," said Robby.

"You're right," agreed Mr. Walter. "I'll tell you what — we'll start doing that, and we'll have an answer for you in a few weeks. Fair enough?"

"Fair enough," replied Robby, and he strode out of the store ahead of his parents, hands in his pockets, face to the sun.

Olivia, Ruby, and Flora pulled three paint cans into a circle near the door and sat down on them.

"Isn't it funny," said Olivia, "how something that seems so bad can turn out to be so good?"

"What do you mean?" asked Ruby.

"When my dad lost his job it seemed — well, not like the end of the world, but pretty bad. I didn't know what was going to happen — whether we might have to move or something — and then Dad couldn't decide what he wanted to do. Now he and Mom are opening their own store, and they seem so excited. Dad never looked excited when he left for the office in the morning. And I'm going to get to help out in the store, and now maybe Robby will get a job here. I don't know if that will actually happen, but still."

"And you'll have the grand opening in just two months," said Flora.

"Hey, Annika will be here then!" exclaimed Ruby. "She'll get to see the store."

And just like that, Olivia felt her mood darken.

"You guys are going to like each other so, so much," Flora promised.

Olivia said nothing.

"Remember the time Annika made the treasure hunt in her attic?" Ruby asked, and Flora grinned. "She was always thinking up good ideas like that," Ruby continued. "Her birthday is in July, and two years ago she had a summertime Christmas party. We sang Christmas carols and made Christmas decorations."

"It was ninety-five degrees outside," said Flora.

"And once," Ruby went on, "she set up a fortune-telling stand in her front yard. I played Madame Zaroka, her helper."

"I took in the money," Flora told Olivia. "We made eleven dollars."

"It took us forever to divide it up, remember?" said Ruby. "Annika and I finally got the extra pennies because we had the hardest jobs."

"You mean, because I'm such a nice, kind person," said Flora.

Olivia wanted to say "I have lots of good ideas, too," but she realized her good ideas mostly revolved around such things as insect behavior and migratory patterns and the windchill factor. Now that Olivia thought about it, even the project she was working on for the town birthday celebration seemed dull. Olivia was taking photos of local wildlife for the photography exhibit. Flora, on the other hand, had embarked on a history project that was turning up all sorts of interesting things about her ancestors in Camden Falls.

Nikki would be able to show everyone what a talented artist she was. And Ruby — well, it was hard to top Ruby's drama-filled role as Alice Kendall, possible witch.

"Olivia?" said Flora. "Are you okay? You're so quiet today."

"I'm okay."

Through the window of Sincerely Yours, Olivia saw the familiar sights of Main Street. There were the trees, some old and grand, some new and spindly, "greening up," as her mother would say. There were the spring's first tourists (Olivia could always tell them from the people who actually lived in Camden Falls), brought out by the fine weather, strolling up and down the street with their shopping bags. There was Jackie, who worked in the post office, and Frank, who owned Frank's Beans. And across the street was Time and Again, the used bookstore, where Olivia bought old books about wildlife, often for as little as fifty cents.

Olivia was trying to see what was in the window of Time and Again when the door to the bookstore opened and Sonny Sutphin wheeled out. He made his way to the corner of Boiceville Road, wheeled himself down the dip in the sidewalk, across to the other side of Main Street, and up another dip. Olivia lost sight of him then, but a few moments later he appeared at Sincerely Yours and steered inside.

"Hi, girls," he said.

"'Morning, Sonny," they replied.

Usually Sonny stopped to chat with them, but this morning he seemed to be in a hurry. "Olivia, are your parents here?" he asked.

"In the back," said Olivia, and at that moment, they returned to the front, having given Dr. Malone, the dentist, a peek at the kitchen.

When Dr. Malone left, Sonny approached Olivia's parents. "I don't know if you'll be hiring anyone to work here after you open, but if you're in the market for help, I'm in the market for a job." He handed Mr. Walter a paper from a stack in his lap and said, "These are my particulars. Please call me if you have an opening."

"Goodness," said Mrs. Walter when Sonny had left. "Two applicants in one morning!"

Olivia knew she should feel excited — about the store, the opening, Robby, Sonny, the fine spring weather — but Annika came into her mind and all she felt was sadness.

# CHAPTER 4

# Aunt Allie

The gentle weather didn't last as long as anybody would have liked, and Ruby was disappointed.

"It's too early for weather that warm. It was bound to turn," said Min sensibly.

"But March is supposed to go out like a lamb," Ruby replied. It was a chilly Saturday morning, and she was not pleased.

"Well, it's not *snowing*," said Flora. Ruby mumbled something crabby and unintelligible, and Flora raised her eyebrows. "Don't you have a play rehearsal all day today?" she asked her sister. "The run-through? I thought that would make you happy."

"It does," said Ruby. "It's just that I wanted to walk to school wearing my new shirt."

"So wear it under your jacket," said Flora.

"That's missing the point!" said Ruby.

"Heavens to Murgatroyd," said Min. "What is *wrong*, Ruby?"

"Maybe I'm a little nervous," Ruby admitted. "Today is our first run-through, but Mrs. Gillipetti called it a stumble-through."

"Ah," said Min, "I see. That implies mistakes."

"And accidents and problems," said Ruby. "A whole Saturday full of them."

"I'll walk you to school," offered Flora. "How's that?"

Ruby brightened. "Okay! Thank you."

"Remember that when you come back this afternoon, Ruby, I'll already be gone," said Min.

Ruby nodded. Min and Mr. Pennington had plans to go to an art exhibit that afternoon. The exhibit was in Charity, thirty miles away, and they were going to have dinner there afterward.

"So Aunt Allie will be in charge this evening," Min continued.

Ruby and Flora exchanged a glance, which they hoped their grandmother didn't see. But nothing was said about their aunt until they had set out for Camden Falls Elementary.

"She's probably going to make us eat okra and cabbage for dinner," said Ruby. "And drink soy milk!"

"But after dinner," said Flora, "she'll fire up her computer and ignore us. Then we can do anything we want."

Aunt Allie, the younger sister of Ruby and Flora's

mother, had come to visit for the holidays a few months ago. Ruby had looked forward to the visit with some excitement. Her aunt, she thought, must live a glamorous life. She was a writer and had an apartment in a high-rise building in thrilling Manhattan. She had even been to Broadway shows, and Broadway was where Ruby herself hoped to be one day. Not sitting in an audience but standing onstage in front of the audience, the more people the better.

Then Aunt Allie had arrived and Ruby's bubble had burst. Her aunt was stiff, she had no sense of humor that Ruby could detect, and her idea of a great present was a check for someone's savings account. Worse, when the holidays were over, Allie didn't seem to be in any hurry to leave Camden Falls and eventually said that she had had enough of New York and wanted to continue her writing career here, where she had grown up. She was house-hunting but hadn't seen anything she liked. The third-floor guest room she occupied was filling with more and more of Allie's things as she made trips to New York, then returned with items from her apartment.

A horrifying thought now struck Ruby, and she said, "Flora, you don't suppose Allie will decide to stay with *us*, do you?"

Flora looked shocked. "In *our* house? I don't think so."

"But it's taking her such a long time to find a place

of her own. She's so picky. And as long as she stays with us, she doesn't have to cook. Min does all the cooking."

"Yes, but she doesn't like what we eat. You know that. We're not organic."

Ruby frowned. "What's wrong with Twinkies, I wonder. Aunt Allie is such a boring adult."

The girls had reached their school by then, and Flora said, "Do you want me to come in with you, Ruby?"

"No, thanks. I feel better. Look, there's Mrs. Gillipetti, waiting for everybody. I'll see you this afternoon."

Ruby and the other cast members, young and old (the youngest ones were kindergartners with their parents, the oldest were sixth-graders), followed Mrs. Gillipetti inside Camden Falls Elementary and through the halls to the auditorium. Ruby knew she was lucky to go to a school with its very own auditorium. Her last school, in her old town, was bigger than CFE but did not have a separate cafeteria and auditorium — just one big room that did double duty. When it was being used as an auditorium, it was hard to ignore the folded-up tables and chairs lining the walls. Also, there had been no stage. Ruby was grateful to have a stage.

"People," said Mrs. Gillipetti as she opened the doors to the auditorium, "please put your coats and things down over there and then take seats in the front. I want to explain what we're going to do today."

In our stumble-through, thought Ruby. She felt her heartbeat quicken.

When the children were seated, Mrs. Gillipetti stood before them and said, "All right. Up until now we've mostly been rehearsing in smaller groups, and we haven't had any run-throughs."

This was true, thought Ruby. The last time the cast had performed the entire play had been just before the holidays, when they'd held a special assembly for their school. Things had not gone well — although Mrs. Gillipetti had retained her sense of humor.

"So now," continued Mrs. Gillipetti, "the hard work begins." She smiled. "But this will be fun, too. You'll get to see all the pieces fall into place. Eventually, we'll be rehearsing in our costumes with the scenery. In fact, we'll start rehearsing with some of the scenery today."

Ruby raised her hand. "Is it finished?" she asked.

"Not all of it. Some of the backdrops are still being painted. But we have Alice Kendall's house as well as John Parson's, and some of the trees have been completed as well. I should add that the group in charge of scenery is going to be working onstage with us today, painting the town backdrop, so you'll have to step carefully. Okay, everybody?

"Now," Mrs. Gillipetti went on, "what I'd like to

do is start at the beginning of the play — the first scene — and try to work through to the very end. I'm going to stop you along the way, probably lots and lots of times. You'll need to make sure you're standing in the right places — that's called blocking — and working with the scenery and the props correctly. Also, think about the costumes you'll be wearing. *And* — this is important — try to say your lines without referring to your scripts. I know this is a lot to remember, but we'll be having plenty of rehearsals between now and May. Okay, everybody who's in the first scene, please follow me onto the stage."

Ruby stood up. As the lead character, she was in nearly every scene in the play.

The run-through began. Ruby had not even finished her first line (which, proudly, she had memorized, along with the rest of the scene) when Mrs. Gillipetti interrupted her to say, "Now, Ruby, you'll be standing over here." Ruby moved a few inches to her right. "No, *here*." Mrs. Gillipetti pointed to a red X that had been taped to the floor of the stage. "You'll all have to watch for your spike marks," Mrs. Gillipetti said, addressing the cast, "so you'll know exactly where to stand."

Ruby started over again with her first line, standing carefully on the X. "Can you say that more wistfully?" Mrs. Gillipetti said. "You have a lot of enthusiasm, and that's good, but this line needs to sound wistful."

Ruby frowned. Wistful? Full of wist? "Wistful" was not on the long list of emotions Ruby felt she had mastered.

"Look as though you long for something," said Mrs. Gillipetti helpfully, and Ruby started over yet again.

Half an hour later, the first scene finally ended. Mrs. Gillipetti had stopped it more times than Ruby could count to point out spike marks, to remind the cast members about props they'd be using, and to encourage memorization of lines. Ruby's stomach was beginning to feel queasy, but when the scene finally ended, Mrs. Gillipetti said, "Bravo!"

Ruby couldn't help herself. "Bravo?" she repeated.

Mrs. Gillipetti smiled. "Now you know what real actors feel like. Good work, people."

Real actors? It was Ruby's turn to smile.

The second scene began. Ruby didn't have quite as much work to do in Scene Two. But in Scene Three she was supposed to cry. Mrs. Gillipetti had told her from the beginning that if she couldn't cry real tears, she could simply cover her eyes with her hands and make sobbing noises. This was not good enough for Ruby. For months she had been working hard at bringing forth tears the first time Alice Kendall is accused of being a witch. Now, when the accusation was made (by Harry Lang, a fifth-grade boy who glared fiercely but not very convincingly at Ruby), she screwed up her face, swallowed hard, bit her lip, and managed to make tears (real tears) spring to her eyes. Harry was so surprised that he was late with his next line, and Mrs. Gillipetti once again said "Bravo!" when the scene was finished. Then she added, "Excellent, Ruby."

The praise was enough to change Ruby's opinion of a stumble-through, and she worked hard the rest of the day, paying careful attention to Mrs. Gillipetti's directions and feeling very professional indeed.

When the long day was over, Ruby left CFE tired but pleased. And she smiled when she turned the corner onto Aiken Avenue and saw the Row Houses. She passed the Morrises', Mr. Willet's, the Malones', then turned up her own walk.

"Hello, everybody!" she called as she flung open the front door.

"Hi!" Flora's voice floated downstairs from her bedroom, followed by Olivia's: "Hi, Ruby!"

Ruby took off her jacket and dropped it in the hallway, thought better of this, and hung it in the coat closet.

Aunt Allie appeared in the doorway to the living room. "Ah, there you are, Ruby. How's *The Witches of Camden Falls* coming along?"

"Good," replied Ruby, remembering the fine moment in which she had stunned the cast with her real tears. "I'm tired, though." She followed her aunt back into the living room and flopped onto the couch.

"Have you done your weekend homework?" asked Aunt Allie.

Ruby closed her eyes. "No." When she heard nothing from her aunt she opened them again. "What?" she asked.

"You'd better get started."

"Now? I just got home. Besides, I can do it all tomorrow. I don't have that much."

Aunt Allie raised an eyebrow. "Ruby. I believe Min said you have a science test to study for."

"Oh, yeah. I forgot. But I can do that tomorrow."

"We're going to be busy in the afternoon, remember? That doesn't leave you much time."

"I'll have all morning! That's enough."

Aunt Allie leveled her gaze on Ruby. "Your schoolwork," she said, "leaves a lot to be desired."

Ruby knew this was true, but she said, "I'm tired. The rehearsal was really hard."

"I think," said Aunt Allie, "that you have your priorities reversed. For heaven's sake, Ruby, *Witches* is just a school play. But your studies are the pathway to the future."

Well.

Ruby could not believe her ears. *Just* a school play? Did Aunt Allie know nothing? This was perhaps the most important thing Ruby had ever done. She was starring in the play. *Starring* in it. As in, playing the most important role. Not only was she learning things such as blocking and how to work with props and scenery (Ruby had been in plays before but never in a production as involved and complicated as this one), but she had to memorize pages and pages of material. And cry! She had to cry! She'd been able to make tears run down her cheeks.

Ruby sat up and glared at her aunt. Wait until opening night, she thought. Ruby would show Aunt Allie that what she had worked so hard on all year long was far from *just a school play*.

Aunt Allie smiled at Ruby as her niece left the living room. "I'll be glad to quiz you on your science chapters," she said.

"Okay," Ruby replied, and she clumped up the stairs. "I'm going to study now." Aunt Allie didn't need to know that she was going to study her lines and not Chapter Eleven in *Our Wide World of Nature*.

# CHAPTER 5

# A Peek in the Windows

If on a fine spring day you were to decide to visit Camden Falls, Massachusetts, you would find a small town with lots of nice shops on Main Street. You could pop into Cover to Cover and buy a book. You could order something to drink (hot or cold) at Frank's Beans. You could backtrack a bit and go to the T-shirt Emporium for an I'VE BEEN TO CAMDEN FALLS shirt. (Nobody who lives in Camden Falls ever wears these shirts, but the tourists like them.) Cross the street and buy an ice-cream cone at Dutch Haus. Check out the local hiking guides in Doubletree Sporting Goods, then admire the window of Needle and Thread, recently decorated with vibrant felt flowers by Flora and Ruby Northrop and Olivia Walter. Continue south on Main Street and you'll pass a store currently being renovated with a sign above the door reading SINCERELY YOURS. A notice taped to the window informs you that the store will open in May and will sell not only candy and baked goods but everything you might need to create a gift basket for any occasion — a birthday, a baby shower, a holiday, a graduation, a retirement. Take out your notebook and write down the phone number and Web address at the bottom of the notice because starting in June, you'll be able to order these gift baskets by phone or over the Internet.

Now, if you head back to the parking lot behind the shops on the east side of the street, you can load your purchases into your car and take a drive in the country. Camden Falls is situated at the foot of some hills (you really can't call them mountains), with flatter country spreading out in other directions. Nikki Sherman and her family live off to the west of town, and to the north-west is the new home of Mrs. Willet. Mary Lou Willet, whose husband, Bill, occupies the second Row House from the left on Aiken Avenue, has been living at Three Oaks for several months now. Three Oaks, Mr. Willet told Min, is what is known as a continuing-care retirement community with apartments for independent living as well as rooms for people who are ill or who can no longer take care of themselves. There's a wing for people with Alzheimer's disease, and this is where Mrs. Willet lives. If you were to peek through her window at Three Oaks on this early spring day, you would find a pleasant room furnished with things from the Willets' house. Sitting on the bed is a teddy bear that Robby Edwards made for Mrs. Willet last fall. She calls the bear Sweetie, which is the name of the Willets' cat, and even though she doesn't know where it came from, she likes it very much, as Robby knew she would. Mrs. Willet herself is not in the room right now. She's down the hall in the Activities Center, making a collage under the direction of Dee, whom Mrs. Willet also likes very much. Her days at Three Oaks are busy. She is especially happy whenever that man who might be her husband arrives for a visit.

Now leave Three Oaks and drive east toward town but turn left onto Aiken Avenue before you reach Main Street. Park your car and study the Row Houses for a moment. There's no other structure like this in Camden Falls. The Row Houses were built in 1882, which was more than fifty years before Min was born, and they consist of eight nearly identical adjoining homes, a solid granite structure almost a block long. The first people to live in these homes were wealthy, and the small rooms on the third floor of each house were occupied by maids. Butlers answered the door, and gardeners tended the yards. Today the houses are still occupied by eight families, but these people tend their own gardens and answer their own doors. The third-floor rooms have become offices and playrooms and nurseries.

Take a peek in the windows to see who lives here now. The house on the left end belongs to the Morrises. They have four children. The oldest are twins, and Lacey is one of Ruby Northrop's good friends. Then there's Travis, who's six, and Alyssa, who's the youngest kid in the Row Houses . . . at least until the Fongs, who live at the other end of the row, have their baby. On this weekday, all the Morris children are in school, Mr. Morris is at work, and Mrs. Morris is answering her e-mail.

Next door to the Morrises lives Mr. Willet. He's been alone since Mary Lou moved to Three Oaks. At first he felt relief when his wife was safely settled into her new home. For more than a year she had been unable to dress herself or take care of herself, and Mr. Willet had been having more and more trouble doing these things for her. Now he misses his wife of fifty years desperately, and his days seem very long and lonely. He's getting ready to visit Mary Lou, which he does nearly every day.

Dr. Malone and his daughters live in the house to the right of Mr. Willet. There's not much to see through their windows just now because Dr. Malone is at his dental office on Main Street, and Margaret and Lydia are at Camden Falls Central High School. Margaret is a junior this year, thinking about going to Mount Holyoke College or maybe Smith College, and she's working hard, especially in her language classes. At the moment, Lydia is supposed to be in her algebra class, but she has allowed herself to be talked into leaving campus (which is forbidden unless you're a senior) and is now walking across the street with her friends to where Bud the hot dog vendor has brought his cart. She can think up an excuse for her math teacher later.

Min, Ruby, Flora, and (for the time being) Aunt Allie live in the house to the north of the Malones. On this morning the only one at home is Aunt Allie. She had intended to spend the hours before lunch revising her latest short story but has abandoned her computer and is on the phone with a real estate agent. Min is working at Needle and Thread with Gigi, and Flora and Ruby are at Camden Falls Elementary. Neither Flora nor Ruby is concentrating on her schoolwork just now. Flora's mind is on her research project, the one she's working on for the town birthday celebration, and Ruby is lost in the world of witches and Alice Kendall. Despite the tears she was able to shed at the rehearsal, she's wondering if her performance was really as good as she thinks it was. Is she *truly* a good actor, or is she just good for a nine-year-old?

Next door to Min's house is the one belonging to the Walters. The Walter children are in school, but Mr. and Mrs. Walter are at home, planning for the opening of their store. They're sitting at the kitchen table together, creating a grand opening flyer. If Olivia could see them, she would think that they haven't seemed so happy in a long, long time.

To the right of Olivia's house is Mr. Pennington's, and today he is in his backyard, feeling as happy as the Walters are. Last summer, when he was having a hard time, he didn't get around to planting his vegetable garden, but this year he's feeling up to it. He's standing by the weedy patch that two years ago was the home to neat rows of lettuce and beans, and he's making a chart of what he'll plant where. He thinks that this summer he might try growing beets. "Is that a good idea, Jacques?" he asks, and Jacques wags his tail.

Robby Edwards and his parents live on the other side of Mr. Pennington's house. Right now Robby is in school and Mr. and Mrs. Edwards are both at work. Robby likes school (even though his special class moved from the high school back to the elementary school last fall), but he's eager to graduate and start working. "I want responsibilities and a paycheck," he tells Mrs. Fulton, his teacher, as they study a math worksheet. "And a girlfriend."

The Fongs live in the house on the right end of the row. They're not home, either, although when they are at home these days they enjoy working on the nursery for their baby girl, who will be born soon. Today they're at their studio on Main Street. They have offered to exhibit the artwork that will be entered in the competition during the town celebration, and they're trying to figure out how to display it.

"Just think," says Mrs. Fong as she eyes their large workspace, "by the time the exhibit opens, our baby will be here."

# CHAPTER 6

# Conversations — Part I

When Flora moved to Camden Falls at the beginning of the previous summer (which seemed now to be both a very long time ago and a very short time ago), there were many days when she wanted to be alone, so she would escape to Min's attic. Eventually, she began to explore it. She had hoped the attic might be like one in a book — hiding a doorway to another world or at the very least harboring a trunk full of treasure. But Min's attic had proven to be of the more boring kind. It held boxes of old clothes (but not even *very* old clothes) and boxes of dishes, plus some furniture of dubious quality that wasn't being used but that Min couldn't bear to part with. At last, though, Flora had discovered a carton holding old letters and keepsakes and papers and journals. Careful examination of some of the letters had led Flora to a mystery. It wasn't, she had to admit, quite as exciting as the mysteries Nancy Drew usually found herself thrust into (often on the very first page of the book), involving spies and thieves and jailbirds. But as homegrown mysteries go, Flora's wasn't a bad one.

Flora had learned that long ago (in 1929, before Min was born) Min's father had done something that had lost a lot of money for a lot of people. A bit of reading had revealed that he hadn't done anything wrong; as a stockbroker he had made investments for his clients, and when the stock market crashed, sending the country into the Great Depression, his clients lost their savings. Those clients had blamed Min's father for their losses, which led to a chain of events that, Flora realized, had affected more than just the people whose investments had been lost. Employers lost their businesses and had to let their workers go. The workers, now with no income, were forced to give up their homes or to find lower-paying jobs. Babies were born into poverty when they once might have been born into prosperity.

Flora's mystery grew more interesting when she learned that Mary Woolsey was connected to it. Mary's father had been one of the people whose money had been invested and lost by Min's father. The fortunes of Mary's parents had changed, so Mary had been one of the babies unexpectedly born into a poor household, her future a question mark. As Flora came to know

Mary better, a new mystery arose. Who had sent Mary anonymous gifts of money for decades after her father was lost in a fire at the factory he'd begun working in after the stock market crash? Mary had thought it was Min's father, acting out of guilt over the changes he'd caused in the lives of the Woolseys. But Flora, feeling like quite a good sleuth, had eventually realized that that wasn't possible, and the mystery remained unsolved, Mary's benefactor a question mark himself. Or herself, thought Flora.

Flora had become interested in how this one moment in the life of Lyman Davis, her great-grandfather, had affected so many other people. Now, with Mary's help and Min's permission, she was doing a project for the town birthday celebration, planning to interview people living today in Camden Falls whose lives had changed because of her great-grandfather. And she was going to start with Mrs. Jacob Fitzpatrick, the woman Mary Woolsey had suggested she visit.

"I've been sewing for her for several years now," Mary had told Flora in Needle and Thread one day. Mary earned her living doing mending and sewing, and several times a week she came to Needle and Thread to pick up articles of clothing that had been left for her or to drop off finished pieces.

"Mrs. Fitzpatrick?" Min said. "Sorry, but I couldn't help overhearing. She's a very nice woman, Flora. Are you going to interview her for your project?"

"I guess," said Flora, suddenly nervous about talking to a complete stranger.

"She'll be perfect," said Mary. "I think you'll see why after you've spoken with her."

Flora looked at Min. "I don't know Mrs. Fitzpatrick at all. I feel funny calling to ask if I can interview her."

"I understand completely," said Min. "How about if I call her for you?"

"Oh, thank you!" replied Flora, who had been afraid that Min might tell her to buck up and face her fears.

So it was arranged that after school on Wednesday, Aunt Allie would drop Flora off at Mrs. Fitzpatrick's house on the eastern edge of Camden Falls and return in thirty minutes to pick her up.

On the appointed afternoon, Flora sat in the front seat of her aunt's car, a notebook and tape recorder in her lap, butterflies in her stomach.

"Wow," she said softly as Aunt Allie drove up a winding drive. A great stone mansion loomed ahead of them.

Aunt Allie stopped the car in front of the house, and Flora reached for the handle of the door, then hesitated.

"Do you want me to come in with you?" asked Allie, and Flora looked at her gratefully. "Or I could wait here in the car."

The door to the house opened then, and out stepped

a smiling woman wearing a tweed suit. "Flora?" she said. "I'm Mrs. Fitzpatrick."

Flora smiled back at her and said to Aunt Allie, "You can go. It's okay. Thank you for driving me here."

"I'll see you in half an hour," Allie replied.

Flora followed Mrs. Fitzpatrick through the doorway, and when she stepped into the grand entrance hall, she turned around and around, like someone in a movie. The hall was bigger than Min's whole living room. Oil paintings hung on the walls, each lit by its own tiny individual lamp. From the center of the ceiling swooped a chandelier decorated with what Flora thought must be hundreds of crystal pendants.

This was the house belonging to the descendant of someone who had lost all his money in the crash of 1929?

"Your grandmother explained your project to me," said Mrs. Fitzpatrick. "Very interesting."

Flora nodded. "Thank you. I didn't know anything at all about my great-grandfather until I moved here."

"Come. Let's sit in the drawing room," said Mrs. Fitzpatrick.

The drawing room. Flora had never met anyone whose home included a drawing room.

Mrs. Fitzpatrick led the way into a lavishly furnished room with floor-to-ceiling windows looking out over a sloping lawn. She indicated a chair, which

Flora sat in, and then she lowered herself into a matching chair.

Flora opened her notebook and said, "Do you mind if I tape our interview?" (Min had told her to say this, adding, "It's rude to start recording without asking first.")

"Not at all," replied Mrs. Fitzpatrick, and Flora switched on the recorder.

Flora, feeling more nervous than ever, nevertheless began the short introduction she had rehearsed. "In nineteen twenty-nine," she said, "my great-grandfather, Min's father, was a stockbroker here in Camden Falls. When the market crashed —"

"I believe that day was called Black Thursday," interrupted Mrs. Fitzpatrick.

"Really?" Flora made a note in her book. "When the market crashed, a lot of my great-grandfather's clients lost their fortunes. Was your father one of them?" Flora was beginning to think that either Mary had made a mistake, or that she wanted to show Flora that some of Lyman Davis's clients had not lost their fortunes and had continued to do well for themselves.

"Yes," said Mrs. Fitzpatrick. Flora looked so surprised that Mrs. Fitzpatrick laughed. "I know. You wouldn't guess it by looking around. But the truth is that my father lost, well, not every penny he had — that would be an exaggeration — but almost all of his money. I wasn't born yet, by the way, so I don't remember any of this."

"Did your family live here then?" asked Flora.

"They lived in Camden Falls but not in this house. They lived in another large house, though. It wasn't quite as big as this one, but it was still a beautiful old home. It isn't too far from your house on Aiken Avenue, Flora. Anyway, by January of nineteen thirty, my father realized just how much trouble our family was in, and according to my older brother, who remembers this night very well, our father sat down at the dinner table one evening and announced that they were going to have to move. He told my mother and my brother that he was going to sell the house and all of their belongings, and that they were going to move in with his younger brother. The next day he called the household staff together and told them the same thing, adding that he would have to let them go."

Flora nodded, thinking of her great-grandfather saying the same thing to Mary Woolsey's mother and the rest of the staff at his house.

"My brother told me," Mrs. Fitzpatrick continued, "that when Father made this announcement, the gardener hung his head, two of the maids began to cry, but the chauffeur smiled."

"Why did he smile?" asked Flora.

"Mr. Pennington? Because he —"

"Excuse me," said Flora. "The chauffeur's name was Mr. Pennington?"

Mrs. Fitzpatrick nodded. "Rudy Pennington, I think. Why?"

"Rudy Pennington is the name of our neighbor!"

"At the Row Houses?" asked Mrs. Fitzpatrick.

"Yes."

"That's the junior Rudy Pennington, then. He's the son of the man who was our chauffeur. And his father was smiling because . . . I'm not sure exactly, but I think he saw losing his job as an opportunity. Flora, if his son is your neighbor, you ought to talk to him, too. I imagine he'll have an interesting story for your project, and a very different one from the one you'll hear today."

"Okay," said Flora, making another note in her book.

Mrs. Fitzpatrick, staring out a window now, said after a moment, "My father was a man of his word. The staff was let go, and he really did sell the house and my family's possessions. But what happened in the next few years was that my father and his brother joined forces to start a store in town. The store thrived, so they opened another store, then bought a third business and more businesses after that. By the time I was a teenager, Father had built this house, and I've lived here since. I taught all my children not only to be smart with their money but to be charitable as well."

"Do your children live in Camden Falls?" asked Flora.

"My daughter does. Sheila DuVane. I'm very proud of her."

Sheila DuVane? Could that be the Mrs. DuVane who had long been helping out Nikki's family? Flora couldn't think of a tactful way to phrase that question, so she made yet another note in her book. Maybe she would ask Min about it later.

Flora looked at her watch. The half hour was almost over. "This has been really interesting," she said to Mrs. Fitzpatrick. "Thank you very much for talking to me. It was actually Mary Woolsey who suggested that I interview you."

"Oh, Mary Woolsey." Mrs. Fitzpatrick stared out the window again. "Now, that was a sad story." Flora was about to ask what she meant by this when Mrs. Fitzpatrick continued. "I suppose you've heard about the fire at the factory."

Flora nodded. "Do you remember it?"

"Not well. I was just a little girl when that happened. But I do remember my mother saying from time to time that after the fire her friend Isabelle was never the same. Isabelle was the sister of Mary's father."

Flora jerked to attention. Mary had never mentioned any relatives, only her parents.

"My mother also said," Mrs. Fitzpatrick went on, "that if someone wanted to leave his life behind and start over fresh, with a new identity, the fire afforded an easy way to do that."

Flora was pretty certain that her mouth dropped open at this remark, but the doorbell rang then, and Mrs. Fitzpatrick rose to her feet, saying, "That must be your aunt."

Flora followed her back to the hallway. The interview was over.

# CHAPTER 7

# Surprise!

"This is the dress for the baby?" said Olivia. "Wow." She was sitting on the floor in Flora's bedroom. The room was a mess, awash in fabric scraps, bits of paper, open books, and pattern pieces. The half-finished dress, which Flora now held out for inspection by Olivia and Ruby, was not the first one Olivia had seen Flora make, but she never ceased to be surprised by what her friend could do.

She touched the front of the dress. "What's that called again?" she asked.

"Smocking," replied Flora.

"I love it." Olivia examined the tiny stitches that formed a picture of the cow jumping over the moon.

"We'd better hurry and finish our baby presents, all of us," said Flora. "The shower's less than a week away."

The Row House neighbors were planning a baby

shower for the Fongs. It was going to be held at Olivia's house, and it was supposed to be a surprise for Mrs. Fong. (Mr. Fong was in on the secret.) Olivia recalled her tenth birthday party, held the previous autumn, which had indeed been a surprise. But adults, she felt certain, were harder to surprise than kids. Still, surprise or not, the shower would be fun, and Olivia, Ruby, and Flora had decided to make their presents for the baby. Now, however, the shower was just days away, and none of their gifts was finished.

"How's your present coming?" Olivia asked Ruby.

"Well . . ." said Ruby.

"You have been working on it, haven't you?" asked Flora.

"Well . . ." said Ruby again.

"Ruby," said Flora.

"We're having a lot more play rehearsals now than before!"

"Okay," said Olivia calmly. "Show us what you've done. Maybe we can help you. I only need a couple of hours to finish my present."

"First let's see yours," said Ruby.

Olivia opened a paper bag and carefully withdrew a package wrapped in tissue paper. "It's a photo album," she said. "I bought the album, but I'm making a cover for it — it's going to say BABY in pink-and-white-checked fabric right here — and I decorated some of the pages. See? Mr. and Mrs. Fong can take pictures of the baby's 'firsts' and put them in the album. This page is for her first walk in her carriage, this one is for her first Halloween, this one is for her first steps. All I need to do now is finish the cover."

"Olivia, that's beautiful! It's a great idea," said Ruby.

"But you're not off the hook, Ruby Jane," said Flora. "Come on. Let's see your present. What have you got?"

Ruby made a face at her sister. Then she left Flora's room, crossed the hall to her own room, and returned a few moments later holding out an empty soup can.

"What's that?" asked Olivia.

"It's a can," replied Ruby.

"We can see that," said Flora.

Ruby sighed. "I figure it could be either a rattle or a piggy bank. I could fill it with pebbles or something and it could be a rattle —"

"You mean a choking hazard!" shrieked Olivia. "That's a terrible idea."

"All right then, a bank," said Ruby. "I'll wrap the sides with construction paper, make a top out of cardboard or something, and cut a hole in it for dropping the money through."

"Why," said Flora, "am I reminded of the pencil cup you made Dr. Malone for Christmas? Oh, that's right. Another decorated soup can."

"Look," said Ruby, growing angrier, "I have play rehearsals and dance classes and chorus rehearsals —"

"You guys, don't fight," interrupted Olivia. "The point is that Ruby needs to make a present. Fast. Flora, you and I have time to help her. Let's all sit down and think."

"How about a stuffed animal?" said Ruby a few moments later.

"That's not a bad idea," said Flora. "We still have a couple of teddy bear kits left at the store."

"Hmm," said Olivia. "I wonder what Annika would make."

Flora frowned. "What do you mean?" she asked.

But Ruby said, "She'd make something wild, like a jungle quilt."

"Is Annika good at sewing?" asked Olivia.

"Pretty good," said Flora. She turned to her sister. "Why don't we call Min and ask her to bring one of the kits home tonight? I can help you with a bear, okay?"

"Okay," replied Ruby.

Olivia and Flora turned to their own gifts, but Olivia's mind was on Annika and jungle quilts and all that Annika had in common with Flora.

Four days later, on a rainy Saturday afternoon, Olivia's house began to fill with neighbors, who arrived through the Walters' back door, bearing packages hidden in grocery bags and old cardboard boxes.

"Not that the Fongs will see us," said Olivia to Flora and Ruby. "They should be in town now. Then at two o'clock Mr. Fong is supposed to say, 'Come on, dear. Let's go home. We'll stop by the Walters' on the way and pick up their old high chair.'"

"What if Mrs. Fong doesn't want to stop by?" asked Ruby.

Olivia's face fell. "I didn't think of that," she said.

"Don't worry," said Flora. "Mr. Fong will get her here one way or another."

Olivia looked around her living room. It was filling up fast with both neighbors and presents. Her mother kept sending out plates of food, which Olivia, Ruby, and Flora were in charge of passing to the guests.

Olivia loved company. There were Mr. Pennington and Min, sitting side by side on the couch. There was Aunt Allie, talking awkwardly to Robby, who was so excited about the surprise that he was bouncing up and down on his toes. "We bought the baby a car seat!" he exclaimed. "It's in that box, that big one over there. It's almost the biggest present of all!" There was Margaret Malone talking to Mr. Willet, and Lydia Malone sitting on a chair in a very bored fashion, sneaking a peek at the texts on her phone, which Dr. Malone had told her not to bring. And there were the Morris kids, chasing Jack and Henry up and down the stairs.

In the midst of the confusion Olivia glanced first at her watch and then through the front window.

Suddenly, she yelped, "I see the Fongs! Here they come! They're almost here!"

The room grew quiet.

"Everyone stand back there," said Mr. Walter, pointing. "And don't say a word," he added, looking deliberately at Jack, Henry, Alyssa, Travis, Lacey, and Mathias, who had screeched to a halt at the bottom of the stairs. "I'll answer the door. When I let them in, yell 'Surprise!' . . . but not *too* loudly."

The Row House neighbors huddled at one end of the Walters' living room, while Mr. Walter waited in the hallway. Ruby suppressed a giggle, Mrs. Morris hushed Travis and Alyssa, and Flora reached for Olivia's hand and gripped it.

Olivia heard the door open.

"Hi," said her father.

"Hi," replied Mr. Fong. "We thought we'd pick up the high chair, if it's convenient."

"Absolutely. Come on in."

The Fongs, Mr. Walter behind them, appeared in the entry to the living room, and Olivia and her family and friends cried, "Surprise!"

Olivia watched Mrs. Fong's face closely and decided she wouldn't be able to look quite so startled unless she was either truly surprised or a very good actor. She actually thought her neighbor seemed just a teensy bit frightened.

Mrs. Fong's hands flew to her cheeks.

"Did we surprise you? Did we surprise you?" asked Alyssa.

"You certainly did," said Mrs. Fong, and she began to smile. "Thank you!" she exclaimed. She turned to her husband. "You knew, didn't you?"

He was smiling, too. "Hardest secret I've ever had to keep."

Mrs. Fong, hands resting on her belly, was ushered to a chair, and the adults began to talk and laugh. Olivia and Flora and Ruby passed the plates of food again, but after just a few minutes, Lacey Morris cried, "Open the presents now! We can't wait any longer."

And so the present opening began.

"I've never seen so many gifts," exclaimed Mrs. Fong.

There were baby blankets and baby socks and baby hats. There was a red wagon from Dr. Malone and a stack of picture books from the Morrises and plenty of handmade gifts, including the album from Olivia ("Stunning," said Mrs. Fong) and the dress from Flora ("You're so talented," said Mr. Fong) and the teddy from Ruby ("Our baby's first stuffed animal," said Mrs. Fong). Min, Mr. Pennington, and Mr. Willet had pooled their resources and bought a baby carriage. Even Lydia had bought and wrapped a crib mobile and seemed genuinely pleased when the Fongs proclaimed it to be exactly the kind their baby book recommended.

When the last gift had been opened, Olivia surveyed the paper-strewn room with satisfaction. Then she glanced at Mrs. Fong and saw tears in her eyes.

"She's *crying*," she whispered to Flora and Ruby.

"Because she's happy," said Ruby.

"Because she's pregnant," said Flora.

Mrs. Fong kept saying "Thank you" and "We're so lucky to have neighbors like you" and Olivia knew the party had been a success.

Later, when the neighbors had left and the mess had been cleared up and the Walters had eaten a haphazard supper of hot dogs and party leftovers, Olivia lay on her bed and thought dreamily of the new baby and what would happen after she was born. With Mrs. Willet at Three Oaks, the Row House neighbors would once again number twenty-five (not counting Flora and Ruby's aunt Allie, who still said she was house-hunting). Funny how things worked. One person left, a new one arrived. And Alyssa Morris would no longer be the youngest Row House kid. Furthermore, by the time the baby was a toddler, Olivia would be old enough to sit for her. In fact, in just over five years, the baby would be ready for kindergarten at Camden Falls Elementary.

At this, Olivia's thoughts ran off on their own and she couldn't seem to reel them in. Thinking of kindergarten made her think of graduation and the fact that her own kindergarten days didn't seem so very far in the past. Graduation reminded her of the things that would happen just *before* graduation — the town birthday celebration, for example, and Annika's arrival. And the thought of Annika led Olivia down paths she'd rather not travel.

Olivia sank onto her bed, and at last she admitted something to herself, something she had been thinking about ever since the day Flora had announced that Annika was coming to visit: Olivia had the horrible feeling that Annika had been a better best friend than Olivia was.

How, Olivia wondered, could she prove that she was a good best friend, too? A creative and talented best friend, as Annika apparently had been?

Olivia's eyes searched her room and they fell on the animal pictures she planned to enter in the photography exhibit.

# CHAPTER 8

# *Dress Rehearsal*

In the months since Ruby and Flora had arrived in Camden Falls, their life with Min had begun to fall into place, and a routine had developed. Part of this routine was doing chores, which (Ruby couldn't help noticing) had not become an issue until Aunt Allie arrived. Ruby wasn't certain who was responsible for the Chore Chart that had appeared on the refrigerator; nevertheless, chores were now a part of her daily routine. Mostly, she didn't mind them, especially since the responsibility for the chores rotated, and there was one chore that she actually liked. Ruby was currently responsible for taking Daisy Dear on her first walk of the day.

Ruby had originally protested, since walking Daisy meant getting up fifteen minutes earlier every morning. But now Ruby felt quite grown-up and responsible as she clipped Daisy's leash to her collar, Min's clock chiming seven in the background, then unlocked the front door of the Row House and headed down the path to the sidewalk. She was the only person on Aiken Avenue at that hour, and she liked the stillness of the street.

Sometimes Ruby talked to Daisy, sometimes she simply paid attention to the gardens and the light and even the air. Once she had been startled to see a nearly full moon hanging over the horizon and had said, "Did you know the moon could shine in the morning, Daisy?"

On a Saturday in mid-April, Ruby made another discovery. "It's warm, Daisy," she said, "really warm." And it was. Not early spring, just-warm-for-a-day warm — but true spring-is-here warm.

That reminded Ruby that her play was only a month away, and she felt a flutter of excitement in her stomach because today was the day of the first full dress rehearsal of *The Witches of Camden Falls*.

"I hope I'm ready," she said aloud, and Daisy turned around to cock her head at Ruby, ears springing to attention.

The dress rehearsal was an important event, even if it was really just a rehearsal at which all the costumes were to be tried on so they could be adjusted before the true dress rehearsal in May. Min and Gigi were going to attend, since they were on the costume committee, so Liz Durbin and Rick O'Bannen would run Needle and Thread that day. Flora was helping with the costumes as well, and since Nikki had been chosen to draw the picture that would be on the cover of the play program, she also wanted to attend the rehearsal.

When Min and Ruby and Flora arrived at Camden Falls Elementary that morning, Ruby drew in her breath. "Look at all the cars in the parking lot!" she exclaimed. "It looks like the whole world is here!"

"It takes a lot of people to put on a production like this," said Min. "There's the refreshment stand and the program and the music, not to mention the costumes and scenery and, of course, the actors."

For just a moment, Ruby felt like a very small part of the play, and she was reminded of nights when she would lie in bed and think about how big the universe was and how small she was compared to infinity. But then she told herself that she was Ruby J. Northrop and she was the star of the production and undoubtedly the most important person at CFE that day.

Ruby put a little skip in her step. "Come on!" she cried. "We have a lot to do." She ran ahead of Min and Flora and flung open the front door of the school. Ruby had every intention of proving to the world that she was a professional actor and that the production of *The Witches of Camden Falls* was more than just a school play.

● × ● × ●

Fifteen minutes later, Ruby was seated in the auditorium with Min, Flora, and Nikki, who had ridden her bicycle to school. The auditorium was crowded with people, and Mrs. Gillipetti was struggling to make herself heard above the din. After clapping her hands and calling "Attention!" to no avail, she whispered something to Harry Lang, who ran to the stage, put his pinky fingers in his mouth, and let out a piercing *"Fweeeeee!"*

Everyone fell silent, and Mrs. Gillipetti said, "Thank you. This is going to be a busy day, so let's get to work."

Ruby jumped to her feet, ready for Scene One, but the next words out of Mrs. Gillipetti's mouth were, "I'd like to start with reports from the committee heads."

Reports from the committee heads? thought Ruby. What about getting the rehearsal under way? But she took her seat again and tried not to wiggle as first one person, then another stood and gave a brief report.

Harry Lang's mother said that volunteers were needed to bake cookies and snacks that could be sold at the refreshment stand, and that other volunteers were needed to provide food for the cast party.

One of Stephanie Ford's dads reported that the programs wouldn't be going to the printer for two more weeks, so there was still time to buy ad space.

Then Mrs. Gillipetti called on the head of the flower committee, and a parent Ruby didn't recognize stood and said, "Jarita's Flowers has agreed to be the florist for the play. Anyone who wishes to send flowers to a member of the cast or crew should call Jarita's a day in advance. The bouquets, with cards attached, will be delivered here, to school, before each performance. The presentation of the bouquets will take place after the curtain call. We'll announce this in the school paper as well as the town paper next month."

Ruby's mind, which had wandered during the talk of snacks and ad space, snapped back to attention at the mention of flowers. Now, *that* sounded professional. She had seen beautiful leading ladies on television receive bouquets of flowers from fans or husbands or parents and thought this very glamorous. Ruby imagined herself onstage in a filmy red dress and red high-heeled shoes (which, she recognized, might be teetery when walking across the stage, but she skipped over that detail), leaning down to accept an armload of yellow roses handed to her by someone whose face could only be described as rapturous. "Thank you, thank you," Ruby would say breathlessly, pretending, for the fan's sake, that this almost never happened, when in fact it happened night after night. Then Ruby would glance into the first row and there she would see Aunt Allie, and only because Ruby was such a good actor would she be able to keep the smug expression from her face.

Ruby felt a poke in her ribs then and realized that Flora was nudging her. "Hey, Rip Van Winkle," Flora said, "wake up. We're supposed to go backstage now so you guys can try on your costumes."

"Can I come with you?" asked Nikki.

"Sure," said Flora. "We need all the help we can get."

That didn't inspire confidence, thought Ruby as she made her way down the aisle toward the stage. "Why do you need all the help you can get?" she asked suspiciously.

"Oh, don't worry. It's just a figure of speech," replied Flora in an annoyingly adult voice.

But Ruby was dismayed when she went backstage and discovered first of all that by "backstage" Flora just meant the corridor and two fifth-grade classrooms, and second that this area was a madhouse.

"Where's my dressing room?" asked Ruby.

"Your *what*?" exclaimed Nikki, and everyone in earshot began to laugh.

Ruby was about to point out that she was the star but instead simply rephrased her question. "Okay, where are *the* dressing rooms?"

"Right here," said Min.

Ruby looked at her grandmother. Min was standing midway between Mr. Levithan's room and Ms.

Holton's room in front of a banner that read THE BOOKWORM BOOK CLUB. Ruby frowned.

"There are no dressing rooms," said Min, turning to send Flora a warning look when Flora threatened to laugh again. "This is just a school play, honey."

"But we have an auditorium and a stage. And there's going to be a refreshment stand. And flowers —"

"But it's still a school," said Min gently, "not a theatre. Now, come on. You need to try on your costume."

"Well, I'm not putting it on out here with all those boys around."

"Of course not. Makeup will go on in the corridor. Girls will change in Ms. Holton's room, boys in Mr. Levithan's room. Okay?"

"Okay," said Ruby glumly. This was not at all what she had had in mind. Maybe for the two actual performances she could find a spot — a utility closet or something — that she could turn into her dressing room. She could even make a gold star to hang on the door.

For the time being she had to be content with standing by the globe in Ms. Holton's room, an eye on the door at all times to make sure no boys peeked in, while Min and Flora fussed with her costume: a long, very plain brown dress; a white cloth cap; a white apron; and a pair of sturdy shoes borrowed from Flora, which were slightly too big, so the toes had been stuffed with tissue. Once the costume was on, and Min had stood back to scrutinize it, Ruby took it off again, except for her shoes and her cap, which Mrs. Gillipetti wanted her to rehearse in. Then Ruby, now wearing the shoes, the cap, her jeans, and a T-shirt, was told to go out into the hall to await her turn in the makeup chair.

"It's going to take hours to put on everyone's makeup!" cried Ruby as she watched from the doorway. "Look. There's just one person doing it."

Sure enough, a woman (Ruby couldn't remember whose mother she was) was painstakingly trying rouge and mascara and powder (making notes as she did so) on every single performer, right down to the kinder-gartners, who, as far as Ruby could recall, didn't even have any lines to say.

"That's why," Min replied patiently, "you'll have to arrive at school a couple of hours before each of the performances. It takes a long time to prepare everyone."

"But in a real theatre," said Ruby, "there would be more than one makeup person. And the star would probably have her own private —"

"Ruby," said Min, "I don't even want to hear the end of that sentence."

Ruby snapped her mouth shut and stalked down the hallway, where she sat by herself on the floor outside the door to the library, glowering, her arms folded tightly across her chest. Not far away, a group of girls, already in costume and makeup, was laughing and playing a complicated clapping game while chanting, "Eeny-meeny DIS-aleeny, ooh, ah, AH-maleeny, atcha-katcha, ooma-raga, ugga-wugga OOH! ISH-biddly oten-doten. . . ." Ruby knew the game and was very good at it but chose to sit on the floor until she was called to the makeup table.

This is all Aunt Allie's fault, Ruby said to herself as she sat sullenly while her makeup (including lipstick!) was applied. Aunt Allie had made her self-conscious. There was really nothing good about Aunt Allie, Ruby decided. Except maybe the fact that she had finally found a house she wanted to buy, which meant that she would soon be moving out of the Row House. Ruby couldn't wait.

Her makeup applied, Ruby again sat alone, but this time she was preparing for her role as Alice Kendall. She stretched a little and did the breathing exercises she had invented. The exercises were supposed to help her concentrate and focus, but Ruby's mind kept wandering and she found herself breathing in rhythm to "Eeny-meeny dis-aleeny, ooh, ah, ah-maleeny. . . ."

Later, when the dress rehearsal was finally under way, Ruby was painfully aware that this time she had more of an audience than usual. Min, Gigi, Flora, Nikki, and plenty of other people were sitting in the auditorium, watching. Ruby did her best all afternoon and even managed to become teary-eyed when the fierce Harry Lang hurled his accusation at her.

But on the way home that evening when Min said, "Ruby, my stars, you were splendid! You really looked like you were going to cry," all Ruby could think was that she *hadn't* actually cried. Not like before.

Her performance was already slipping. She was washed up before opening night.

# CHAPTER 9

# *Conversations — Part II*

Flora had listened to the tape of her interview with Mrs. Fitzpatrick twice and then had spent several hours writing down most of the conversation. ("That's called transcribing," Aunt Allie had told her, and she should know, since she was a writer.) Flora now realized that she was going to have to have a conversation with Mary Woolsey — possibly an uncomfortable one — about Isabelle, Mary's aunt, and about people leaving their lives behind and starting over with new identities.

Flora had also been looking through the notes she had made during the last few months when she had spoken with Mary or Min about Lyman Davis. And she had hauled the box of family papers out from under her bed and read through the letters several more times. But she still didn't have a clear idea of what she was going to do with all the information. How could she present her project to the Camden Falls Historical Society so that it could be displayed at the town birthday festivities? A report wasn't all that interesting, she thought, picturing some of the reports she'd handed in to teachers over the years — stapled together at one corner or (when she was younger) stuck between sheets of red construction paper. Flora wanted her part in the festivities to be memorable. After all, this was Camden Falls's big birthday, and Camden Falls was now Flora's home.

Ruby's part in the festivities would most certainly be memorable. And Nikki's drawings would be framed and displayed in an actual art gallery, while Olivia's photos would be mounted and displayed at another gallery. But where was Flora's research leading? What was she going to do with her pile of letters and hours of transcribed tapes?

Flora didn't know, but for once she decided not to worry. Her next interview was with Mr. Pennington, and she needed to concentrate on that. On a Monday afternoon, she returned from school, called hello to Aunt Allie, who was clacking away at her computer, grabbed her notebook and tape recorder, and walked across Olivia's yard to Mr. Pennington's house.

She rang the bell and immediately heard frantic barking and the sound of Jacques lumbering into the hallway, skidding on a rug, and banging into the doorjamb.

The barking continued at a furious level until Mr. Pennington opened the door.

"Hello," he said, smiling. When Jacques saw Flora, he fell silent, then sent his tail flapping back and forth like laundry in the wind.

"Hi," Flora replied. She bent to pat Jacques.

Mr. Pennington ushered Flora inside and said, "I feel honored to be interviewed. Where shall we sit?"

"Anywhere is okay as long as I'm near an outlet," Flora answered. "I need to plug in the recorder. Is it okay if I tape the interview?"

"Yes, it is. Thank you for asking," said Mr. Pennington, and Flora had a feeling that Min had already mentioned the recorder to him.

Flora and Mr. Pennington sat down in the living room, Flora in an armchair and Mr. Pennington on the couch with Jacques beside him. Jacques fell asleep in an instant and was soon snoring loudly.

Flora had been in Mr. Pennington's house many times, and the living room was her favorite room of all. It was filled with more books than Flora had ever seen in one place except a library. The room was lined with shelves that extended from the floor all the way up to the ceiling, and every inch was occupied by books. They were tightly packed but orderly, and Mr. Pennington now told Flora that they were organized by a system and that he could locate any of his books in a matter of moments. "Fiction is over there," he said, pointing, "poetry is there, drama there, and non-fiction is divided into lots of categories. There are biographies, autobiographies and memoirs, history, science. All alphabetized according to the author's last name. A number of the history books cover the Depression," he added, "which my family spent in a somewhat unusual manner, compared to other families, but I don't want to get ahead of myself. This is your interview, Flora."

Flora made her rehearsed introduction about Lyman Davis, then added, "When I was talking to Mrs. Fitzpatrick, she said that after her father lost his money, he had to let his staff go, and that one of those people was his chauffeur, Rudy Pennington. I said that a Rudy Pennington was my neighbor, and she guessed that you're Rudy Pennington Junior. Is that right?"

"It is. In nineteen twenty-nine, my father was employed as the Fitzpatricks' driver. It wasn't uncommon for white families, even those who lived in the North, to employ African-American help, only back then those workers were called the colored help."

Flora cringed. "Should I put that in my report?" she asked.

"You don't like that term, do you?"

"No." Flora felt uncomfortable.

"Well, it's up to you, of course. But it is the truth."

Flora changed the subject. "Mrs. Fitzpatrick also said that when your father was let go, he smiled."

Mr. Pennington grinned. "I don't know whether he did or not, but that's a nice touch for your report. And it certainly could be true, because my father always said that the best day of his life was the day he lost that job."

"But why?"

"Because it was holding him back. My father was lucky to have a good job, especially with a family to support, and he was grateful for it. But, Flora, do you really think he wanted to be a driver all his life?"

"No," said Flora, who, in truth, could think of lots of jobs she wouldn't want, certainly not for her entire life.

"And it wasn't just that driving was boring and a dead end. It was much more than that. There was something my father wanted desperately."

"What?"

"Look around the living room. Can you guess?" asked Mr. Pennington.

Flora looked at Jacques, at the tables holding the familiar framed family photographs, at the shelves and shelves of books, at the case she knew contained Mr. Pennington's trumpet.

"A nice life and a nice house?" she guessed, fairly certain that this wasn't the answer Mr. Pennington was leading her toward.

"That might have been part of it, I suppose," said Mr. Pennington kindly, "but what he really wanted,

Flora, almost more than anything except his wife and children, was an education."

"Oh," said Flora, and then, "*oh.*"

"Do you understand?"

"Yes."

"When the Fitzpatricks let my father go, he suddenly saw that he had the freedom to do whatever he wanted."

"But he was free already, wasn't he?"

"Well, yes, technically he was a free man. But his job had been holding him back because it was comfortable. Now, my father thought, as long as he had to reshape his life, he might as well take the opportunity to find a way to do what he'd always dreamed of — to get an education. So he packed us up and we moved in with his parents, who lived a few miles outside of Camden Falls. Imagine seven people crowded into a house that was small to begin with, but my grandparents were very kind, and they supported my father's decision. Dad spent the next few years in school, while my mother and my grandparents worked at whatever jobs they could find.

"Eventually," Mr. Pennington continued, "my father graduated from college. He was the first person in his family to do so, and we had a big celebration. Oh, I remember that day. I don't think you've ever seen anyone more proud than my grandparents, my mother, my brothers and I, and, of course, my father.

"Later, Dad became a college professor himself. When I grew up, I went to college in Pennsylvania, but I wanted to come back to this area. I moved to Boston first, and then after I got married, my wife and I moved here. That was when I began teaching at your school, Flora."

"And then later you became the principal of the central school, right?"

"Exactly right."

How different, thought Flora, were the Depression years for Mr. Pennington and his family than for Min and her family, for the Fitzpatricks, or for Mary Woolsey and her family.

"Mr. Pennington," she said, "do you know of any other people who were affected by Min's father? I mean, by losing their money or getting fired or something?"

Jacques rolled over on his back and Mr. Pennington rubbed his belly. "Well, let me see. There was the gardener at the Fitzpatricks'. I recall that after he lost his job he led a rather exciting life. He hit the road, doing a little work here, a little work there, to earn pocket money, catching free rides on trains whenever he felt like moving on."

"You mean he became a *hobo*?" exclaimed Flora.

"I suppose so. Not a life I would have liked, but he did get to see the country. Then there was a man, Johnny something, who was part-time help at the

Fitzpatricks' and who was a friend of my father's. I remember my dad saying one night after we had moved in with my grandparents that Johnny still hadn't found another job, and I don't think he ever did. A year or so later his wife left him and finally he just dropped out of sight.

"Oh, and I can think of someone else you might be interested in hearing about," said Mr. Pennington, shifting on the couch when Jacques rolled over again. "My mother knew Sonny Sutphin's grandmother." (Flora raised her eyes and looked at Mr. Pennington with increased interest.) "The Sutphins were a respectable family in Camden Falls, what you'd call middle class nowadays. They didn't have a lot of money, but they were doing fine, and your grandfather had invested their savings. They lost it all in nineteen twenty-nine, but quite unexpectedly they came into a large inheritance in nineteen thirty or thirty-one and were then far wealthier than they'd been before the crash."

Flora thought of Sonny in his shabby clothes, wheeling himself up and down Main Street every day. She thought of his tiny, dark apartment, which she'd visited with Mr. Pennington before the holidays. "What happened?" she asked. Surely the Sonny she knew now didn't have any large inheritance.

"The money was spent rather" — Mr. Pennington paused — "*erratically*. It really was a great deal of money and it caused some wild behavior in subsequent generations of Sutphins. When Sonny came into his portion of the inheritance, the first thing he did was spend most of it on a fancy car — maybe a Porsche, I'm not sure — and he hadn't had it very long when he was in a horrible accident. He was driving way too fast and he crashed the car late one night. His brother was in the car, too, and he was killed."

"Oh," said Flora in a very small voice, imagining not Sonny and his Porsche but her family and their car on that snowy evening. "Is that how Sonny got hurt?"

Mr. Pennington nodded.

Flora tried to collect her thoughts, which were tumbling around in her head. She was glad the tape recorder was running because she was having trouble keeping track of all the people Mr. Pennington had mentioned. There was the hobo (an actual hobo — very exciting), and the man who wasn't heard from again, and now Sonny Sutphin and his family. And, of course, there was Mr. Pennington himself. What would have happened, Flora wondered, if the Fitzpatricks hadn't lost their money and Mr. Pennington's father hadn't lost his job? Flora might not even know Mr. Pennington. He might never have moved to the Row Houses. Flora couldn't imagine the Row Houses, or her life now, without Mr. Pennington.

Later, when Flora was leaving, she stood on tiptoe and threw her arms around her neighbor. It was time to go home to transcribe their talk and to think about what on earth she was going to say to Mary Woolsey when it was time for their formal interview. Mr. Pennington had started to close the door behind Flora when he stuck his head outside and said, "By the way, what are you going to do with your information, Flora?"

"I'm not sure," she replied.

"What about making a book? I think you're going to have enough material. You could bind your research into a book."

A book, thought Flora. Could she really write a book?

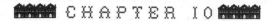 

# CHAPTER 10

# A Stitch in Time

Nikki Sherman was pedaling fast. She liked the stretch
of road that led from the end of her drive, through the
countryside, and into Camden Falls, and she was happy
for an opportunity to ride her bicycle to Needle and
Thread. The sun warmed her hair, making it smell of
moss and wildflowers and springtime. On either side
of the road, oaks and maples dipped their branches in
the breeze, their new leaves a haze of green against the
gold of the sun. Nikki felt as if she were flying along
through a dreamworld.

She reached the top of a small hill and, as soon as
she was coasting fast enough, stuck her legs out straight
as she sailed toward the bottom. She considered remov-
ing her hands from the handlebars but decided against
that, remembering the cautionary tale her mother had
often told her and Tobias and Mae about the time

when she was eight and decided to coast down a hill with her hands held high — and wound up falling off the bike and breaking her wrist. The thought zipped through Nikki's mind — a blip only — and she turned to other matters, her hands gripped firmly around the bars.

It was a fine Sunday, and Nikki had left a happy household behind. By making a down payment provided by Mrs. DuVane, who was a high school classmate of Nikki's mother and who periodically stepped in (not always tactfully) to help out the Shermans, Nikki and her family were now the owners of their first computer. Nikki was excited, although she did not think that buying things over time was a safe way to shop. She knew too well that payments could mount up and bills could become overwhelming. But her mother had insisted, saying that while she was grateful to Mrs. DuVane for the down payment, she was determined to provide for her family. Nikki could hear her unspoken words as well — that her mother was determined to do what her father had not done.

In any case, the computer was going to be a great help with Mrs. Sherman's résumé, with college applications (if Tobias decided to take that step), and with Nikki's homework and even Mae's. When Nikki had hopped on her bicycle twenty minutes earlier, her mother and Tobias had been sitting together at the kitchen table, studying the computer manual, while Mae played with Paw-Paw.

Her family, Nikki realized, seemed complete without her father, and she hummed as she pedaled toward town.

Flora and Olivia had asked Nikki if she wanted to spend the afternoon at Needle and Thread. The Camden Falls birthday celebration was drawing closer, and preparations were under way at the store for two exhibits: one of antique quilts and one of new quilts to be entered in a contest. Furthermore, Min and Gigi were readying the Needle and Thread float for the town's parade.

Flora was terribly excited about the quilt exhibits. "You should see what people have been making. All these cool patterns — kaleidoscopes and wedding rings, log cabin blocks, all kinds of stars. Some of the patterns are *so* intricate. And the color palettes . . ."

Nikki tried to look interested when Flora started talking about the quilts, but every time the subject came up, she could feel her mind drifting. The float was a different story. It was to depict colonial women and girls at a quilting bee. So not only did a colonial scene have to be created for the float itself, but colonial costumes had to be made for everyone who would be riding on the float. Nikki liked the challenge of turning the flatbed of a truck into the setting of a seventeenth-century quilting bee. Even working on the costumes sounded like fun.

Nikki zoomed onto Main Street, then slowed her pace and walked her bike along the sidewalk. She waved to the Fongs through the window of their studio. She felt in her pocket for money to buy a soft drink as she passed the grocery store, but her pocket was empty. She peered through the open doorway of Sincerely Yours but saw only a couple of stray workmen, so she continued on her way, past Heaven, past Zack's, and then she was standing outside Needle and Thread. She locked her bicycle to a metal grate under the window and stepped through the door.

"Hi!" called Olivia and Flora.

"Hi!" said Nikki. "I'm here to help."

Flora remembered how timidly Nikki used to enter Needle and Thread, as if she weren't sure she had a place there. But now she strode inside and flopped down on one of the couches. "What do you want me to do?" she asked.

"Help us with Lacey's costume," replied Flora.

"Lacey's? Lacey Morris is going to be on the float?"

"Yup," said Olivia.

"And who else?"

"Min and Gigi," said Flora.

"Ruby and me," added Olivia.

"And Mrs. Morris," said Flora.

"That's a lot of costumes," said Nikki.

"I know," Flora replied. "It's going to be a really good float. Annika will be so impressed. When we're watching the parade, I can say to her, 'I helped to make all those costumes.'"

"You can also say," said Olivia, "'My best friends helped me, too.'"

Nikki saw Flora glance at Olivia and frown. "Sure," said Flora.

"All right. So what are we doing here?" asked Nikki.

The girls headed for the table at the back of the store. Nikki looked at the partially finished dresses and aprons and hats laid out there; at lengths of fabric, some with patterns pinned to them; at cards of snaps and rolls of elastic.

"Did people have snaps and elastic and stuff back then?" she asked.

Flora shrugged. "We want the costumes to be — what's the word?"

"Authentic?" suggested Olivia.

"Yes, authentic," said Flora. "But they're only going to *look* authentic. We're going to cheat a little."

"Take a few shortcuts," said Olivia.

"Speaking of which," said Flora, "Nikki, let me show you something really cool about elastic."

Nikki and Olivia smiled at each other. Only Flora could think anything about elastic was cool.

"Okay," said Flora. "We need to gather the bottom

of this cap. I don't know how they did it in the olden days, but we could do it by making a casing using single-fold bias tape. See? You sew the casing down along the sides so that it forms a sort of tunnel. You leave it open at both ends and you thread a short piece of elastic through it — shorter than the rim of the cap. Then you anchor the elastic at each end, and just like that the cap is gathered!"

"Wow," said Nikki politely.

"Okay. That's cool enough, but watch this." Flora held a very narrow piece of elastic aloft. "I'm going to sew *this* piece directly onto the edge of this sleeve. *But, Flora, you're wondering, how are you going to do that? The sleeve is so much longer than the piece of elastic.*"

Nikki concentrated fiercely on the sewing table, afraid that if she looked at Olivia now they would both start to laugh.

"Well, it's kind of like magic," Flora continued. "Sewing magic. You just keep stretching the elastic out toward you as you go, and when you reach the end of the elastic and the other side of the sleeve, the sleeve is already gathered. Isn't that great?"

"It's — it's fantastic," said Nikki, still staring at the sleeve. "But I think that if you want me to do something on the costumes it should be a little simpler."

"Hmm," said Flora. "Do you know how to make a hem?"

Nikki thought of the mending basket in their kitchen. Mending was the kind of sewing she did best, having been in charge of the Shermans' mending for many years. Nikki was an expert at letting down the hems on Mae's clothes so she could wear them until she was too big for them or until they fell apart, whichever came first.

"That's what I do best," said Nikki.

"Oh, good," said Flora. "Because our machines can do hem stitches, but sometimes you have to turn hems up by hand. Oh, oh! Wait! This is even better. Nikki, do you know how to make a blind stitch?"

"Cover up its eyes?" said Olivia from the other side of the table, and Nikki finally began to giggle.

Flora looked hurt, though, and Olivia said, "I'm sorry. It's just that you get so excited about sewing."

"Not any more excited than you get about fishers, or whatever those rodents are."

"They're not rodents, they're from the class Mammalia!" exclaimed Olivia.

"Who even knows about stuff like that?" asked Flora.

"Well, who knows about casing tunnels?"

"They're not casing tunnels, they're just casings."

"Excuse me," said Nikki, "but if you two are going to fight, I might as well go home."

"No, don't go!" cried Olivia and Flora.

"Okay, good, because I thought this was going to be

fun. The three of us sitting here working on the costumes together. Please show me what a blind stitch is, Flora, so I can get to work. Okay?"

"Okay," said Flora.

Olivia brushed her hand discreetly across her welling eyes before she looked down at Flora's nimble fingers.

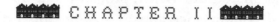

# CHAPTER 11

# Welcome, Baby!

The newest Row House resident arrived on a Tuesday, two weeks earlier than anyone had expected. When Barbara Fong felt the first of her labor pains, she was home alone, her husband having traveled to Boston for the day. This was not how Barbara and Marcus had planned for the baby to arrive. Marcus was supposed to be at home, ready to rush his wife to the hospital, where he would stay at her side until their daughter was born.

But now here was the pain, and there was no point in wishing things were happening otherwise. Barbara gripped the edge of the kitchen table, then looked at her watch. It was just past three in the afternoon and she needed someone to drive her to the hospital. Who in the Row Houses would be home at this hour? Rudy

Pennington and Bill Willet, probably, but if Barbara's husband couldn't accompany her on this extraordinary trip, then what she really wanted was the comfort of another woman, preferably one who had given birth herself. Paula Edwards would be at work now, and so would Min Read. Elise Morris might be at home, but she had young children, and there wasn't time for her to find a sitter.

Barbara picked up the phone and dialed the Walters' house.

"Hello?" said Olivia.

"Olivia? This is Barbara Fong. Is your mother at the store?"

"No, she's right here. Hold on," replied Olivia.

Olivia held the phone toward her mother. "It's Mrs. Fong," she said, cupping her hand over the mouthpiece, "and she sounds kind of excited or breathless or something."

"Barbara?" said Olivia's mother. "Is everything all right?"

Olivia stood inches from her mother, wishing desperately that the Walters didn't have a family rule about eavesdropping on telephone extensions.

"Oh!" said Mrs. Walter a moment later. "All right. First of all, everything is going to be okay. Try to relax. I'll be there as soon as I can, in just a few minutes. I'll call Jackson and ask him to come home from the store. Olivia can hold down the fort until he gets here. . . . What? Your bag? All right, in that case, I'll bring Olivia with me to help pack. The boys can go to the Morrises' until Jackson gets home. Do you want me to call your doctor? . . . Okay. See you in a few minutes."

Olivia felt her heart begin to pound. "Is the baby here? Is she here?"

"Well, almost," her mother replied. "Mrs. Fong is having labor pains. She could be in false labor, I suppose, but we can't take any chances."

"Where's Mr. Fong?" asked Olivia.

"In Boston for the day. Hang on a minute while I call your father."

Mrs. Walter reached her husband, then hung up and said to Olivia, "Okay, your father is going to leave right away. Now, I need you to do two big favors for me, honey. Run the boys over to the Morrises' and ask Mrs. Morris to watch them just until your father gets here. Then meet me at the Fongs' and help me get Barbara ready to go to the hospital."

"Are you supposed to call her doctor?" asked Olivia, already halfway up the stairs to the second floor.

"No, she'll do that. . . . Where's my pocketbook? . . . Oh, here it is. All right. I'm going to drive our car around to the street and park in front of the Fongs'. I'll see you in a minute."

Olivia ran the rest of the way upstairs, collected Henry and Jack, hurried them to the Morrises' house, and explained to Mrs. Morris what was going on. Then she dashed to the other end of the Row Houses and, finding the front door ajar, let herself inside, calling, "Hello?"

"We're in the living room, Olivia," her mother replied.

Olivia suddenly felt nervous. She had been only four years old when Jack was born, and she didn't remember much about the event except that Gigi had moved in for several days and had let Olivia and Henry eat pizza every night.

Olivia peeked around the corner. She saw Mrs. Fong sitting on the couch, breathing rapidly, legs splayed in front of her, hands resting on her enormous belly. Mouse and Rosie, the Fongs' young dogs, sat close by, staring into Mrs. Fong's face. Mouse rested one paw on her arm.

"Honey, run upstairs to the bedroom," said her mother.

"There's a suitcase behind the door," Mrs. Fong added, gasping. "I'll tell you what to put in it."

Olivia listened closely, ran up the stairs, packed the bag as fast as she could, and returned to the living room. Her mother had helped Mrs. Fong to her feet and was now leading her to the front door.

"Follow us out to the car," said Mrs. Walter.

Olivia did so, then ran ahead of them as they approached the sidewalk and opened the car door for Mrs. Fong, tossing the suitcase onto the backseat.

"Olivia," said Mrs. Fong, "could you feed the dogs before you leave?"

"What do I feed them?"

"There's dry food" — Mrs. Fong stopped to draw in a sharp breath — "dry food in a bag in the cupboard by the sink. Just fill the bowls that are on the floor. I called Marcus on his cell phone and he's already on his way back. He'll meet us at the hospital in a few hours. The dogs should be all right until he gets home. Remember to lock the door behind you when you leave."

"Okay," said Olivia. She stood on the sidewalk and watched as her mother helped Mrs. Fong into the car and drove briskly down Aiken Avenue. Olivia returned to the house, feeling very important. She found the dog food in the cupboard, poured a generous amount into the bowls, filled a third bowl with water, then returned to the living room, where Mouse and Rosie were waiting warily on the couch.

"It's okay," Olivia said to them. "Really. I left food for you in the kitchen, and guess what, pretty soon you'll have a new baby sister."

Olivia turned the lock in the Fongs' front door, ran through the yards to her house, and immediately phoned Needle and Thread. "Gigi!" she exclaimed. "Mrs. Fong is having her baby! I have to tell Flora!"

Olivia repeated the news to Flora, then phoned Nikki. "Nikki! Mrs. Fong is having her baby!"

That evening, shortly after Olivia and her father and brothers had finished their dinner, Mrs. Walter returned. Olivia, Henry, and Jack crowded around her as she stood in the hallway.

"Is she here yet?" asked Henry. "Is the baby here?"

"What did they name her?" asked Olivia.

"What does she look like?" asked Jack.

"She looks like a *baby*, stupid!" exclaimed Henry.

"I'm not stupid!"

"Boys," said their father.

Their mother began to laugh. "Just a minute. Let me hang up my coat. Now, come into the living room with me." She sat on the couch and Olivia and her brothers piled on after her.

"Okay," said Mrs. Walter. "No, she's not here yet, but Mr. Fong is at the hospital now, and I think the baby will be born pretty soon. I expect we'll get a phone call tomorrow morning before you go to school. Olivia, I'll need you to walk Mouse and Rosie, since Mr. Fong decided to spend the night at the hospital. Now— homework time and bath time and then into bed."

Olivia felt as if she barely slept that night, and in the morning she was up before her alarm clock went off. She fed and walked Mouse and Rosie in record time and charged back to her house, arriving just as her father was putting breakfast on the table.

"Did they call while I was gone? Did they call?"

Olivia's father smiled at her mother. "Yup."

"Well, what did they say? What did they name her? Don't keep me in suspense."

"Mr. Fong said," Mr. Walter replied in a maddeningly slow manner, "that Mrs. Fong and the baby are both fine, and that the baby's name is . . . hmm. I seem to have forgotten. Now, what was it? Dear, do you remember?"

Mrs. Walter frowned fiercely.

"Stop kidding!" cried Olivia. "Just tell me!"

"The baby's name is Grace," said Mr. Walter.

"Grace," repeated Olivia. "Oh, I like that. And when will she come home?"

"Tomorrow morning, probably."

"Then I'll get to see her after school. Oh, I can't wait!"

Grace Fong had been at home for exactly three and a half hours when she got her first visitors. Olivia, Nikki, Flora, and Ruby arrived at the Fongs' front door on Thursday afternoon, carrying a giant card they had made at Needle and Thread after school the previous day.

Mr. Fong ushered the girls inside, smiling, his finger to his lips, and Olivia and her best friends tiptoed into the living room, where the baby was asleep in a cradle. They stood in a semicircle around the cradle and peered down at the bundle of blankets inside. Grace was wearing a tiny white cap. A fringe of black hair showed beneath it.

Olivia let out her breath. "Welcome, baby Grace," she whispered.

# CHAPTER 12

# Conversations — Part III

Mary Woolsey's house had become one of Flora's favorite places in Camden Falls. Flora had visited it in all sorts of weather. She had sat in the tiny parlor in autumn with red and gold leaves drifting past the windows, in winter with a fire going to keep out the chill as the wind whistled down the chimney and around the corners, on rainy days when Mary turned on all the lamps to dispel the gloom, and on sunny days when Mary opened the windows to let in the breeze and the scents from her gardens.

Today the air was soft and gentle, carrying the fragrance of early lilacs. The curtains waved languidly in the breeze, and no lamps were needed because the sun burned brightly.

"We ought to sit outside," said Mary, who was ready to be interviewed by Flora.

Flora looked longingly at Mary's gardens. "I need to plug in the tape recorder, though," she replied. "Anyway, if we stay inside, I can pat Daphne and Delilah."

"Sleepy creatures," said Mary fondly, stroking the two old cats. "All right. We'll sit inside. I'll make us some tea before we start."

When the tea was ready, Mary brought it into the parlor on a large tray. "Have some cookies first, Flora, and tell me what's going on. Do you have any news?"

Flora reached for a gingersnap, which she knew Mary had made herself. "Well," she said, "Aunt Allie bought a house."

"Did she, now?"

Flora nodded.

"And where is it?"

"Here in Camden Falls. Aunt Allie drove Min and Ruby and me by it the other day. It's really nice. It's old, I think. Like maybe colonial? And it's pretty. I don't remember the name of the road it's on, but it's about ten minutes from the Row Houses."

"When will she be moving in?" asked Mary.

"In June. At least, that's what she's hoping for. She said these things never go as planned. But anyway, she's going to New York City again soon so she can pack up the rest of her stuff." Flora paused and reached for a second cookie. "You know, I'm still not sure why she decided to move back here. It seemed so sudden."

"It's possible that something happened," said Mary. "Something she doesn't want to talk about. But it could also be that she just wanted to come home. Sometimes our roots have a pretty strong pull."

"Do you think," said Flora, "that you can have roots in a place that *isn't* the place where you were born?"

Mary considered this. "I do. Roots are about family, but they can also be about location. Each person has to find the place that calls to him."

"I came to Camden Falls because of the accident," said Flora, "but I think maybe this is also the place that calls to me."

"Well, I'm very glad of that." Mary smiled at Flora, then said briskly, "Now, let me clear away the tea things, and we'll get started."

Flora sat beside Daphne and Delilah and stroked their silky heads. She thought again about Mrs. Fitzpatrick's words and about what she knew she must say to Mary this afternoon. She decided to save that for after the interview, however. And she would turn off the tape recorder then, since this was Mary's private business.

Mary returned to the parlor and sat in the armchair, and Flora switched on the recorder. "This is actually a little silly," she began. "I mean, interviewing you is silly, since I know your story already. But I want to be able to use your words when I write my — my . . . Did I tell you that Mr. Pennington thinks I should write a book? An actual book? Well, not a book like Aunt Allie writes, one that she sends to her publisher and then lots of copies of it are printed up and sold in stores. But Mr. Pennington told me that if I type my project on the computer, I can take the pages to this place on Boiceville Road and they'll bind them in a real cover — a hardcover with the title and BY FLORA MARIE NORTHROP printed on it and everything."

"Oh, Flora, what a wonderful idea!" exclaimed Mary.

"I know. And then the historical society can put the book on display. Imagine. A book with my name on it."

"Maybe you'll be a writer like your aunt one day," said Mary.

"Maybe. Okay," said Flora. "Even though I know it, could you please tell me your story, starting when your father had the job in town and your mother was working at Min's house?"

Mary folded her hands in her lap and drew in a breath. "All right. I'll start in the fall of nineteen twenty-nine. As you said, my father had a job then, and it was a good one. He worked in an office, and later my mother used to tell me proudly that there had been the opportunity for him to advance. Between his pay and the wages my mother earned as a maid for your great-grandfather, my parents were doing fairly well for a young couple. They already owned this house, and the plan was for my mother to work until just before I was born, then to stay at home with me. By that time, they thought, my father might have been given a raise. Plus, there was their nest egg — their savings, which my father had turned over to your great-grandfather to invest. They would dip into that, if necessary, to tide us over until my father earned a larger salary.

"But," continued Mary, "the best-laid plans..." She shifted her gaze from her folded hands to Flora's eyes. "The stock market crashed that fall, several months before I was born. Your great-grandfather let my mother go, but far worse, my parents lost their savings — the money they had been counting on — and then my father lost his job, too, when his employer had to shut down the business. So... no jobs, no savings, and I was on the way. By the time I arrived, my parents had little except this house. Neither of them had been able to find another job, mostly because there were so many people who, like my parents, were out of work. And there were few jobs available, since so many businesses had closed. It was a long time before my father found work at the factory, and it certainly wasn't the sort of job he'd been seeking. But he was in no position to turn it down."

"Do you remember the day of the fire?" asked Flora.

Mary shook her head. "I was only about two years

old. But my mother sometimes talked about the day. She would talk about it the way people talk about September eleventh now, because it was the worst tragedy she could remember, and it affected so many people in town. She would start off by saying that the day was beautiful. It was an early summer day, very warm, with a clear blue sky. She always mentioned the clear blue sky, I think because when the fire started burning, the sky became smoky for miles around. Even people in other towns could smell the smoke. As soon as word spread about the fire, the families of the factory workers began gathering to wait for news. My mother joined them, but she left me with a neighbor. She waited outside the factory for hours, then came home and waited some more."

Mary stopped talking, so Flora said, because she had heard Mary say this before, "And your father never came home. Right?"

"Right. My mother checked at the hospital, of course, and at hospitals in other towns. But my father wasn't located, and . . . he never came home. So my mother and I put together a life for ourselves. We weren't wealthy, but we didn't do badly. I think you know the rest of the story, Flora."

Flora switched off the recorder. "Yes. Thank you for telling me this part in your own words. When I go home, I'll write them down."

Flora set the recorder on a table, along with her notebook. She looked out the window, looked at the cuckoo clock on the wall, watched Delilah twitch in her sleep. Flora opened her mouth, then closed it. She drew in a breath, tried to speak, but instead reached over to scratch Daphne, who had rolled onto her back and was purring loudly.

"Flora? Is there something you want to say?" asked Mary.

"Yes. But I don't know how to say it." Flora retrieved her notebook and turned to the pages on which she'd taken notes when she interviewed Mrs. Fitzpatrick. "I have to tell you something," she said at last.

"All right," said Mary gently.

"When I talked to Mrs. Fitzpatrick," Flora began, "she said something . . . I really don't know how to say this."

"Please. Just tell me what she said."

"She said that her mother had a friend. Isabelle. Does that name sound familiar?" Mary shook her head. "She said Isabelle was your father's sister."

Mary frowned. "That would make her my aunt. But I didn't think I had any relatives, apart from my mother."

"And she said," Flora continued, "that after the fire, Isabelle was never the same."

"What did she mean?"

"I'm not sure, but then Mrs. Fitzpatrick told me that her mother used to say . . ." Flora stopped again. "This is the hard part. She said her mother used to say that if someone wanted to leave his life behind and start over, like with a new identity, the fire would have been a good way to do that."

Flora looked anxiously at Mary, searching for signs that she had upset her friend. She saw instead that Mary's lined face had softened.

"Ah," said Mary. "I understand."

"You do?"

Mary stood and crossed the room to a littered desk. "I have something to show you." She ignored the papers spilling off the surface of the desk and opened a drawer. She withdrew a sheet of blue stationery. "I found this several months ago," she said, "with some of my mother's things." Flora glanced at the page, and Mary explained, "It's a letter from my father to my mother. And it's dated nineteen thirty-five. That was three years after the fire."

"Oh!" Flora let out a gasp. "So . . . you knew?"

"I'd begun to suspect. The letter confirmed it. I think," said Mary, "that my father took the fire as an opportunity to escape a life that had become overwhelming for him. I'm not trying to excuse what he did but to understand it. And I don't think he was a bad man, just confused. After all, he helped support me after he left."

"He did?" said Flora. "How?" And then in a flash all the pieces fell together. "You mean *he* was the one who sent you the money?"

"I think so," said Mary. "I'll never have proof. The letter mentions money but nothing specific."

"I don't understand. Why didn't your mother tell you your father was alive?"

"I think she was trying to spare me. She didn't want me to know he'd abandoned me. She was in touch with him, though. Probably for years."

"Huh," said Flora. "I wonder about Isabelle. It sounds like she lived in Camden Falls or nearby. I wonder if she kept in touch with her brother. She was probably horrified by what he had done. But he *was* her brother."

"I don't know. I'll have to talk to Mrs. Fitzpatrick. Isabelle wouldn't be alive now, of course, but perhaps Mrs. Fitzpatrick knows something more."

"Maybe," cried Flora with sudden enthusiasm, "Isabelle had children! You might have cousins, Mary. You might have a whole, big, huge family! And they might know what happened to your father. It's kind of exciting."

Mary smiled, and Flora felt deeply satisfied. A mystery — a decades-old mystery — had been solved. And Flora was writing a book. She tried to picture it on display at the historical society. Then she tried to picture Annika's face when she saw it. The book would establish Flora's place in Camden Falls. It would say that she belonged here as surely as busy Ruby, who had found a place for herself here months ago, or as surely as Olivia or Nikki or anyone else who had been born in Camden Falls. Flora couldn't wait for Annika to see her project.

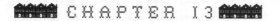 

# CHAPTER 13

# Murphy's Law

Spring that year, the year Camden Falls turned 350 years old, was the loveliest Nikki could remember. This was partly because of the fair weather, and partly because Nikki had friends, and partly because there had been no word from her father since Christmas, so Nikki could truly enjoy everything. She enjoyed playing in the yard with Paw-Paw without having to listen for the sound of her father's truck grinding along their drive. She enjoyed reading in bed late at night against a backdrop of peepers and owl calls instead of raised voices from the kitchen. She enjoyed drawing and being able to leave her work lying out in the open.

Furthermore, every time Nikki walked down Main Street, she saw new signs of the town birthday festivities. This was all very exciting until the week before the big event. It was then that Nikki learned a new term: Murphy's Law. She heard it first from Min.

On a spectacularly bright and sparkling afternoon, Nikki walked into town after school with Olivia, Ruby, and Flora, as she often did now, having asked Tobias to pick her up at Needle and Thread on his way home from work later that day.

"Isn't it beautiful?" Nikki exclaimed, throwing her arms out and tipping her head back. "Isn't everything beautiful? Isn't everything great?"

Olivia and Flora and Ruby smiled.

"You're crazy," said Ruby.

"Nope. Only happy. Look — Main Street is getting dressed up."

"It *is* exciting," said Olivia as they watched a crew of workers setting out pots of flowers along the sidewalk.

Already lights had been twined around lampposts and outlined most of the store windows. "Just like at Christmastime," said Ruby.

"Min drove us by the fairgrounds on Saturday," said Flora. "The tents are going up. Oh, I can't wait for the fair. I hope there will be candy apples."

"And cotton candy," said Ruby.

"Balloons," said Nikki.

"Games with prizes," said Olivia.

"Maybe I'll win a stuffed animal," said Flora. "I never win stuffed animals. Only plastic necklaces."

"I want to win a goldfish for Mae," said Nikki.

"I want to go on rides," said Olivia. "Do you think there will be rides?"

Nikki shook her head. "I don't know. Probably. I like bumper cars and the Ferris wheel."

Nikki sighed, thinking of soaring through the air. Then she thought of hot dogs and corn on the cob and fireworks and the ring toss and the china smash. She hoped there would be a china smash. She also hoped to be able to go to the fair at night, when everything would be glowing and twinkling. She'd been saving her money for weeks.

"Look!" exclaimed Ruby as they passed Dutch Haus. A sign had been placed in the window. It read HAVE A SUNDAE NAMED AFTER YOU! DRAWING TO BE HELD MAY 24TH! ENTER INSIDE. "I want a sundae named after me," said Ruby. "It could be made with strawberries and pink ice cream, because of my name."

Across the street in the windows of the real estate agency were photos not of houses for sale but of Camden Falls homes over the years, going back more than a century. "Hey," said Flora, "there are the Row Houses in eighteen ninety-four."

Nikki and her friends wandered up Main Street as far as the Cheshire Cat, crossed back to the other side, and walked down to Needle and Thread. It was when they entered the store that Nikki learned about Murphy's Law.

"Hi, Min!" Ruby and Flora called to their grandmother.

"Hi, Gigi!" Olivia called to her grandmother.

Their greetings were answered with grunts.

"What's the matter?" asked Olivia.

Min and Gigi were at the table in the back of the store, the costumes for the parade float spread before them. "Not a single costume is ready," said Min. "This one needs hemming." She paused. "This one needs an entire *dress*."

"This one needs trim that we don't have in stock," said Gigi.

"Less than a week to go. Well, that's Murphy's Law for you," said Min.

"What's Murphy's Law?" asked Nikki.

"'If something can go wrong, it *will* go wrong,'" quoted Min darkly.

"Well, I don't think you should say that!" exclaimed Nikki. "It sounds like bad luck."

And maybe it was.

The next afternoon, Nikki, Olivia, and Flora peeked in at Ruby's play rehearsal. They were standing at the back of the auditorium, commenting on Ruby's ability to cry real tears (which she seemed to have perfected), when John Parson's house fell over. It fell, luckily, in such a way that it crashed down all around Ruby but didn't touch her, since she was in the path of the open window. When the crash subsided, Ruby was left standing in a little open square, surrounded by the mangled house.

"Uh-oh," said Olivia.

Flora and Nikki smothered giggles.

"Ruby! Are you all right?" cried Mrs. Gillipetti.

Already, three sixth-graders had rushed to the house and were trying to stand it up again.

"I'm fine," said Ruby. "But look! Look at the house."

As it was righted, the door fell off. Then the house wobbled and tumbled over in the other direction.

"It's ruined!" exclaimed Ruby.

"It isn't ruined," said Mrs. Gillipetti calmly. "It just needs some shoring up."

Ruby made a face and stomped off the stage.

"What's her problem?" asked Nikki.

Flora frowned. "I don't know. She's really touchy about the play these days. I guess she's nervous."

"Murphy's Law," said Olivia under her breath.

The girls tiptoed out of the auditorium. They headed for town, checked in with Min and Gigi at Needle and Thread, and continued down the sidewalk to Sincerely Yours.

"Wow," said Nikki as they stepped inside. "I can't believe your store is almost ready, Olivia."

Gone were the piles of lumber, the cans of paint, the drop cloths and coils of wire. In their places were gleaming shelves stocked with toys and trinkets for the gift baskets and a polished counter for displaying Mrs. Walter's candies and baked goods.

"Here's everything you need to create any kind of basket," said Olivia proudly. "For instance, how about a birthday basket? You could put candles and blowers and this little book in it, along with chocolates and caramel popcorn. Or you could put together a basket for a new baby with a rubber ducky and a washcloth and a rattle and pink or blue chocolate. The chocolate would be for the parents," she added unnecessarily.

"This is *so* cool," Nikki was saying, and at that moment, from the back of the store, she heard a small crash.

"Mom?" called Olivia. "Dad?"

Mr. Walter emerged from the kitchen a moment later, grumbling mightily.

"What happened?" asked Olivia. "Are you all right? Is Mom all right?"

"We're fine," said her father. "But we're going to have to replace part of the refrigerator."

"Part of the refrigerator!" exclaimed Olivia. "But . . . how long is that going to take? The opening is in three days."

Mr. Walter didn't reply, just turned grimly to the Yellow Pages.

"We *have* to be ready for the grand opening," Olivia said urgently to her friends. "Oh, *why* did Min mention Murphy's Law?"

"I told you it was bad luck," said Nikki.

Not until that evening did Nikki experience Murphy's Law for herself. It happened during the quiet hour after dinner when, on school nights, Mrs. Sherman engaged Mae downstairs so that Nikki could have time alone in their room before Mae went to bed. On this evening, Nikki needed to make the final selection of her drawings for the art exhibit. Previously, she had narrowed them down to six, but each entrant was allowed only three pieces of work, so Nikki needed to weed out three more. This was not going to be easy.

Nikki sat down at her desk. Her drawings, her best ones — actually, they were the best of the best — were now kept in a folder in the top drawer. Nikki opened the drawer.

The folder was gone.

Nikki frowned. She opened the other drawers. She looked under the books and papers on her desk. She looked in the top drawer again, even though there was no way she could have missed the folder the first time.

"Mom!" yelled Nikki, and she began to search her room. She looked on her dresser and then on Mae's. "MOM!" she shouted again. She looked under her bed. She looked under Mae's bed. She had begun to search places in which she was quite certain she wouldn't find the folder (such as Mae's treasure box, which was smaller than the folder), when Mrs. Sherman appeared in the doorway.

"Nikki, what's wrong?"

"My drawings are gone! The whole folder is gone!"

"What drawings?" her mother asked. "What folder?"

"My best drawings. I keep them in a folder, and I was going to choose three of them for the exhibit. But the folder is missing."

"Are you sure? Where do you —"

"I'm positive," Nikki interrupted her mother. "I keep the folder in my top drawer and it isn't there. Mom, I've been working on these drawings *all year*." Nikki's thoughts swooped around in her head like bats at twilight. Maybe her father had returned when no one was at home. He had stormed through the house, had searched Nikki's room, and had found the folder. Nikki imagined her father tearing the drawings into confetti-size pieces and scattering the pieces through the yard.

Her mother's voice interrupted her thoughts. "Well, all right. First of all, try to calm down. Let's think. When was the last time you put the folder back in the drawer?"

Nikki closed her eyes and concentrated. "On Monday," she said. "I looked at them after school. Then I called Olivia to ask her a question about the art exhibit, but she wasn't home, so I put the folder back."

"And you didn't take it out again after that?"

Nikki shook her head fiercely.

"Are you *sure*?"

Nikki started to shake her head once more, but then she said, "Oh, wait!" and she could feel herself beginning to blush. "Um, I took the folder to school on Tuesday so I could show the drawings to Olivia and Flora."

Mrs. Sherman tried to hide a smile.

"I think they're in my desk," said Nikki sheepishly. "I mean my desk at school."

The next day, Nikki ran to Mr. Donaldson's room, searched her desk, and retrieved the folder. All the drawings were safe and sound. That afternoon, Ruby reported that John Parson's house had been fixed. Later, Olivia discovered that the refrigerator at Sincerely Yours had already been repaired. And when the girls arrived at Needle and Thread, Gigi said, "Liz and Rick are coming in for a full day to do nothing but finish the costumes. And the trim we needed arrived on the UPS truck at lunchtime."

Nikki whispered to her friends, "The curse of Murphy's Law is over."

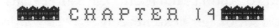 

# CHAPTER 14

# The Grand Opening

"I can't believe it's here," said Olivia at breakfast on Friday morning. "It's here. It's really here!"

Nobody had to ask her what she meant. While most residents of Camden Falls had been waiting over a year for Saturday, the first day of the town birthday festivities, Olivia and her family had been waiting for Friday.

Sincerely Yours was going to hold its grand opening.

"You won't do anything until after school, will you?" asked Olivia anxiously. "Henry and Jack and I have to be there."

"And I get to cut the ribbon," said Jack, even though he wasn't certain what that meant.

"The ribbon-cutting ceremony was announced in

the paper this week," said Mrs. Walter. "It's supposed to take place at three-thirty. So go to the store right after school and you'll be there in plenty of time."

"And when the ribbon has been cut, then Sincerely Yours will be officially open," said Henry.

"People can start shopping!" exclaimed Olivia.

"This weekend is going to be so much fun," said Henry rapturously. "The parade on Saturday."

"And the judging of the exhibits," Olivia added. "Then the fair on Sunday."

"And no school on Monday!" exclaimed Jack. "Can we go to the fair two times? Can we go on Sunday and again on Monday?"

"We'll see," said Mr. Walter.

"We'll definitely go at least once," Mrs. Walter promised.

Olivia's excitement was dampened only briefly when she thought about Annika and her parents, who would arrive later that day. But Olivia had a plan in place. All she needed was a little luck.

After a school day that had seemed unbearably long, Olivia, Nikki, Ruby, Flora, Henry, and Jack left Camden Falls Elementary, crossed Aiken Avenue, and turned the corner onto Main Street. Ahead of them was Sincerely Yours, and in front of the store was a large crowd of people.

"Will you look at that?" said Olivia, drawing her breath in sharply.

"Are they all there for the opening?" asked Ruby.

"I guess so," said Olivia, feeling a flutter in her stomach.

"Come on!" cried Henry, and the children ran the rest of the way to the store, sneakers pounding along the pavement.

An enormous sign in the window read GRAND OPENING in letters painted garishly by Olivia and her brothers. And strung from one side of the store to the other was a wide red paper ribbon.

"Is that the ribbon I'm going to cut?" Jack asked.

"Yes," replied Olivia.

"But why?"

"Why what?"

"Why is there a ribbon and why do I cut it?"

"It's sort of a ritual. It's a way of presenting our new store to everyone," Olivia explained. "You cut the ribbon, like opening a present, and then everyone goes inside to celebrate with us."

"Oh," said Jack.

At three-thirty, Olivia, her parents, and her brothers stood in the open doorway to Sincerely Yours, the ribbon separating them from the crowd of people, larger now than before, standing expectantly outside. At the very front of the crowd were Flora, Ruby, Nikki, Min, and Gigi and Poppy. Just behind them were plenty of Olivia's Row House neighbors — Mr. Pennington, Mr. Willet, several of the Morrises, even the Fongs with baby Grace.

Olivia's parents held up their hands and the crowd grew quiet.

"Thank you for coming," said Mrs. Walter.

"This is a special day for our family," added Mr. Walter.

Olivia smiled self-consciously at her friends.

"We want to welcome you to Sincerely Yours," Mrs. Walter continued.

"And to tell you how happy we are to be part of the Main Street community," said Mr. Walter. "And now, without further ado . . ."

Olivia's father handed Jack a pair of scissors, and Jack snipped the ribbon neatly in two. "We are officially in business!" Mr. Walter said as the ends of the ribbon drifted to the sidewalk.

The crowd applauded, and Ruby put her fingers in her mouth and whistled shrilly. Then, as Olivia watched proudly, her family's store filled with its very first customers.

"Have some candy," said Mrs. Walter, passing around plates of chocolate-covered pretzels and peanut-butter-filled chocolates, then a plate of chocolate threes and fives and zeros in honor of Camden Falls.

"What a wonderful store!" Olivia overheard a woman (someone she had never seen before) say.

"My nephew's graduation is coming up," said Dr. Malone, who had run across the street from his dental office. "Margaret and Lydia could put together a basket for him. That would be perfect. A bookmark and maybe a pen."

"And look," said Olivia, who knew she was going to enjoy helping out in the store, "here are picture frames and mugs with graduation tassels on them."

"Very creative," said Dr. Malone.

Olivia turned to her mother. "I think I just made a sale," she whispered.

The store was bustling. Mrs. Grindle from Stuff 'n' Nonsense was sampling something called chocolate bark. "Very tasty," she said.

Min was eyeing a shelf of miniature books and saying to Flora, "Your aunt Allie's birthday is next month. We should make a basket for her. She'd like this tiny book of poetry."

"And caramel popcorn," said Flora.

Ruby, who was listening, said, "She won't want caramel popcorn."

"She might!" exclaimed Flora. "What if it's organic?"

"Well, here's the beauty of Sincerely Yours," said Min, unperturbed. "We can fill an entire basket without putting any food in it."

Olivia was showing off the case of candies and cookies to Mr. Pennington when Sonny Sutphin wheeled into the store. Olivia turned to look at him and allowed her mouth to drop open.

"What is it?" asked Mr. Pennington.

Olivia stood on tiptoe to whisper in his ear, "I've never seen Sonny in a suit before."

"Well, I'll be," said Mr. Pennington.

Sonny, wearing a smile but somehow looking serious at the same time, approached Olivia's father. "Could I speak with you and Wendy for just a moment?" he asked.

"Of course."

The Walters stepped to a quiet corner and Sonny followed them. "I have news," he said. "And it's both good and bad."

"Okay," said Mr. Walter.

"Well," said Sonny, adjusting his tie, which he was unaccustomed to wearing, "I've been offered a job."

"Why, that's wonderful!" exclaimed Mrs. Walter.

"Thank you," said Sonny. "It's at Time and Again, and I'm very excited about working there. But it means," he continued, "that I won't be able to work here. I want you to know how grateful I am that you even considered giving me a job. Not everyone would take a chance on me. Anyway, I just wanted to tell you, since I know you need to hire someone soon."

"Thank you," said Olivia's parents, and Sonny reached out to shake their hands.

Sonny left the store (eating a chocolate number five), and Olivia was about to find Flora and Ruby and Nikki to tell them the good news, when she caught her parents glancing at each other, her mother with raised eyebrows.

"What?" Olivia asked. "What is it?"

Her parents glanced at each other again, and then her father said, "Okay, but this is a secret for now, Olivia. Understood?"

"Understood."

"We've been thinking about how we want to staff the store, and we planned to offer a job to either Sonny or Robby, but we hadn't been able to decide between the two."

"Now the decision has been made for us," said Mrs. Walter.

"You mean Robby gets the job?" tried Olivia.

"Yup."

"Excellent!"

"But remember, not a word. Not yet," said Mrs. Walter.

"Maybe the Edwardses can come over this evening," added Mr. Walter. "We can talk to them then."

Olivia clasped her hands together. "I hope so," she said.

At seven-thirty that evening, when the Walters' doorbell rang, Olivia, already in a great state of excitement over the successful opening of Sincerely Yours, shrieked, "It's Robby! I'll get it! I'll get it!"

"No, me!" shouted Henry and Jack.

Olivia and her brothers ran to the front hall from three different directions, reached it at the same moment, and fought briefly over the doorknob. In the end, Henry was the one who turned it, and he flung open the door.

There stood Robby and his parents.

"Robby!" cried Jack, and Olivia nudged him, a not very subtle reminder that the news of Robby's job was still a secret.

"Hi," said Robby, and he and his parents stepped through the doorway.

Mr. and Mrs. Walter ushered everyone into the living room. When the Edwardses were seated, Mrs. Walter said, "Robby, as you know, our store opened today."

"Yes. I ate a number three," said Robby.

Mrs. Walter smiled. "We haven't forgotten about your job search," she said. "And now we'd like to offer you a position at Sincerely Yours."

Robby turned to his parents in amazement. Then he leaped off the couch and jumped up and down in the middle of the living room, hands flapping. "A position!" he exclaimed. "A position at Sincerely Yours! It's my dream come true! I can do anything. I can stock shelves. I can talk politely to customers. I can make change." Robby dropped onto the couch again, clapped his hands for a moment, then thrust his fist in the air.

Mr. and Mrs. Edwards were grinning. "Can you wait until school lets out before Robby begins work?" asked his father.

"Of course," said Mrs. Walter.

"We have a number of details to figure out," added Olivia's father. "Robby's hours, his duties. Maybe we'll think about a little training first. But we wanted Robby to know that if he's still interested in the job, it's his. What do you think, Robby?"

"I accept!"

Olivia looked at her smiling friend and at his parents, whose eyes were bright with tears. Then she glanced out the window and saw a car pull up in front of Flora and Ruby's house.

Annika, thought Olivia.

Annika had arrived.

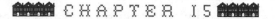 

# CHAPTER 15

# *Flora on Parade*

When the doorbell rang at Min's house, it caused as much commotion as the Edwardses' ring had caused at Olivia's. Flora and Ruby jostled each other down the stairs and crashed into the door, just as Daisy Dear scrabbled around the corner like a cartoon dog, barking at top volume, hackles raised.

"Land sakes," murmured Min.

"Annika! It's Annika!" cried Flora, and she opened the door with a flourish. For a moment she viewed Annika and her parents as if they were a tableau, posed on the front stoop like a scene from her past. Annika's grin, which she had flashed at countless long-ago birthday parties and soccer games and sleepovers, now spread across her freckled face. Her parents stood behind her, hands on her shoulders, but what Flora saw was the Lindgrens watching from their front porch as Flora

**133**

and Annika wobbled along the sidewalk on new two-wheelers; the Lindgrens welcoming Annika's guests to her eighth birthday party; and Mrs. Lindgren rushing into the hospital the night Flora's parents were killed.

Flora swallowed an unexpected sob, then pulled Annika to her and hugged her fiercely.

Ruby elbowed in for a group hug, and soon everyone was hugging.

"I'm so glad you could come," said Min finally.

"We've been waiting forever and ever," exclaimed Annika.

"Come upstairs and see our rooms," said Flora. Her tears had vanished and excitement was taking hold.

"We have to show her downstairs first," said Ruby. "We have a butler's pantry! But no butler."

"We have to show her the whole house," said Flora.

"But we have to do it quietly," whispered Ruby, "on account of Aunt Allie."

"Olivia is right next door," announced Flora.

"Olivia, who's your new best friend?" said Annika.

"Yes. Olivia Walter," Ruby replied. "Her bedroom is on the other side of mine."

"Girls, let Annika and her parents settle in first," said Min. "Have you eaten dinner?"

"We ate at McDonald's!" said Annika. "It was great."

● × ● × ●

That night, when Mr. and Mrs. Lindgren had settled into the remaining guest room on the third floor, and Annika was nestled on a cot in Flora's room, Annika whispered into the dark, "This is so different."

"What is?" asked Flora.

"Everything. Your house — what do you call it?"

"The Row House?"

"Yes. The Row House. It's like you live in an apartment building."

"I guess," said Flora. "But it's still a house."

"And Camden Falls is so . . . so . . . Was that the whole town? What we saw when we drove down that little street with the stores?"

"Pretty much," said Flora. "I mean, there are houses scattered around, and there's our school and the high school and stuff."

"Do you *really* like living here?"

"I really do," said Flora. "Wait until you meet our friends. I e-mailed you about Nikki —"

"Your other new best friend?"

"Yeah. She lives out in the country. And then here at the Row Houses are the Fongs. They just had a baby. And next door on the other side of us live these two teenage girls. One of them is nice. Well, I guess the other one is okay. And the Morrises have four kids. And then there's Mr. Pennington and Mr. Willet. Oh, and here's a cool thing — Olivia says the attics of the Row Houses are connected, but the doorways are hidden and no one has ever found them.

"And wait until tomorrow," Flora went on, beginning to feel sleepy. "You are so lucky to be here for the celebration. The first thing will be the parade. That's in the morning. Then will come the judging of the contests. On Sunday the fair starts —"

"Flora," Annika interrupted, "don't you miss your old life?"

"I miss it every day," said Flora drowsily. She thought she heard Annika mutter, "You'd never know it," but she might have been dreaming.

In the morning, Annika seemed to be in a better mood. Flora awoke to hear her friend exclaim, "Look out your window! I can see a fire engine and a float of some kind. Oh, and a horse. I see a horse!"

Flora leaped out of bed and stood next to Annika at the window. "Gosh, they're lining up for the parade already. What time is it?" She peered at her watch. "Eight-thirty! Annika, we have to get going. The parade starts at ten, and I'm supposed to help Min and Gigi with the float at nine." Flora glanced out her window one more time. "Good. It's sunny," she added. "Perfect festival weather."

"Are you going to ride on the float?" asked Annika.

"No!" Flora yelped. "I haven't changed that much.

But Min and Ruby are going to be on it, and I promised to help them get everything set up."

Flora and Annika dressed in a flash and ran downstairs to the kitchen. They found Annika's parents, Min, Aunt Allie, and Ruby eating a hasty meal of toast and cereal.

"There you are, girls," said Min. "I was wondering when you were going to join us. You must have stayed up late last night."

"Kind of," admitted Flora.

"Well, grab something to eat, and then, I'm sorry," said Min, turning to address the Lindgrens, "but Flora and Ruby and I will have to hustle. You're welcome to join us, or you can come later with Allie."

"I want to go with you," said Annika. "I want to help with the float."

Fifteen minutes later, Min, Flora, Ruby, and Annika hurried out the door and down Aiken Avenue. They passed the fire engine. They passed the horse (his mane splendidly braided). They passed a troop of Girl Scouts. They passed the Turbo Tappers from Ruby's dance school and the Central High marching band before reaching the Needle and Thread float. There were Gigi, Olivia, Mrs. Morris, and Lacey.

"Olivia!" called Flora. "Come meet Annika."

Olivia had been climbing onto the float. Now, with great deliberation, she slid back down to the sidewalk.

She was wearing her colonial dress, a baseball cap, and sneakers. Flora smiled at the sight of her friend, but when she looked from Olivia to Annika, she saw passive, unmoving faces.

"Olivia," said Flora, "this is Annika. Annika, this is Olivia."

"Hi," said Olivia, addressing the sidewalk.

"Hi," said Annika, addressing a hedge.

After that, nobody said a word. Flora marveled at how long five silent seconds could seem. "Um," she said uncertainly.

"Olivia!" called Gigi from the float. "Please come up here. I need your help. And you must take off that cap and put on your proper shoes."

Olivia cast a dark glance at Annika, then turned and resumed climbing onto the float.

"What do you want me to do, Min?" asked Flora.

"Help me with the bunting," was Min's prompt reply. "You, too, Annika, if you don't mind. It's supposed to be draped around the float, but it's coming off for some reason."

Flora and Annika joined Min, and Flora tried to put Olivia and Annika out of her mind. It wasn't hard. There were all sorts of distractions. She saw Bud with his hot dog cart. She saw a man holding an enormous bunch of balloons and wearing a sandwich board that read BIRTHDAY BALLOONS — $2.00! Each red, white, and blue balloon was attached to a stick and bore the number 350. Presently, Sonny rolled into view, his wheelchair decorated with streamers and crepe paper flowers. On the tray of the chair, and in bags attached to the arms and back of the chair, were Camden Falls souvenirs for sale — whistles and bumper stickers and baseball caps and toys and postcards.

Flora forgot about her friends' testy meeting. "This is so exciting, Min!" she said as she held up a length of bunting, which Min attacked with a staple gun.

"It is, isn't it, honey?"

"Look, Annika," said Flora. "There's Bud. He owns the hot dog cart. And that's Sonny over there. Oh, and here comes the Good Humor truck! Hey, did you know that after the parade Ruby is going to perform with the Children's Chorus? They're going to sing on the square in town. And we'll have refreshments —"

Flora was in the middle of this sentence when she and everybody else on the float realized that Lacey was crying.

"What's the matter, sweetie?" asked Lacey's mother.

"I want to watch the parade," said Lacey tearfully.

"But you're going to be *in* the parade."

"I know. But now I want to watch it. If I'm in it, I'll miss everything."

"Lacey," said her mother, a warning note in her voice, "it's a little late for this."

"But I really, really want to watch the parade."

Lacey looked down at Alyssa, Travis, Mathias, and her father, who were on their way to Main Street, where, Lacey knew, her brothers and sister were going to sit on the curb with their friends and cheer and clap as the parade passed by. Lacey wanted to be with them. She wanted to gaze down the street for the first glimpse of the first float. She wanted to feel the drums pounding in her stomach before she even saw the marching band.

Slowly, Lacey began to remove her costume.

Mrs. Morris looked helplessly at Min and Gigi.

"I guess we could do without her," said Min.

"But it's a waste of a perfectly good costume," said Gigi. "And it was made just for her."

"I wonder if someone else could fit in it," said Mrs. Morris.

Min, Gigi, and Mrs. Morris all turned to Flora.

"No!" shrieked Flora. "Not me."

"Please, honey," said Min. "The costume will only be a bit too small, and you'll only have to wear it for half an hour or so."

Flora thought of all those eyes trained on her. She winced. But she said bravely to Min, "Okay."

"Excellent," cried Olivia. "Now you're going to ride up here with me."

"Annika?" said Flora. "You can watch the parade with your parents and Aunt Allie, okay?"

Annika's response was a rather Grinch-like face. "Fine," she said, and she turned and headed back to the Row House.

"Fourth from the left!" Flora called after her.

"Here's my costume," said Lacey gaily as she jumped off the float. She handed a wad of clothes to Flora.

And that was how Flora Marie Northrop, the shyest person in the sixth grade at CFE, wound up riding down Main Street in front of hundreds upon hundreds of pairs of eyes. Later, whenever she thought back on this momentous weekend, she found that she had only the vaguest images from her time on the float — Mr. Pennington waving to her from the sidewalk in front of Frank's Beans, the lighted window of Stuff 'n' Nonsense, the sound of Nikki's surprised voice calling to her (although she couldn't pick her out of the crowd).

What Flora remembered much more clearly was the Needle and Thread float coming to a halt at the south end of Main Street an instant before she shed her costume and said to Min, "Meet you at the square in time for Ruby's concert." Then she grabbed Olivia by the hand and said, "Come on. Let's go find Annika. We have to show her our town."

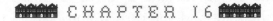 

# CHAPTER 16

# Prizes

Mae Sherman looked with wonder at Main Street. It had been closed before the parade and now, the parade over, it was still blocked off between Aiken Avenue and Stanworth Drive. Not a car was in sight. But plenty of people, old and young, some in costume, roamed up and down and across the street in the warm sun. Quite a few dogs were out, too. Mae saw one at the end of a leash made of red, white, and blue beads. In front of the movie theatre, a man dressed in clothing from the 1890s was playing the piano, and a barbershop quartet was singing "In the Good Old Summertime." Across the street, a vendor was selling peanuts and lemonade.

"Is this a circus?" Mae asked, sniffing the air. She was walking hand in hand with her brother and sister,

Mrs. Sherman just ahead, and she tilted her face up to Nikki.

"It feels like a circus," Nikki agreed. "But it's really a birthday party for our town."

"I liked the parade," said Mae. "Who was that on the last float? Tell me again."

"Uncle Sam," Tobias supplied.

"We have an uncle Sam?"

"No, Uncle Sam represents the United States."

"What?" said Mae.

"Never mind," said Nikki. "Wasn't it fun seeing Flora and Ruby and Olivia in their costumes?"

"Yup," said Mae, skipping a little. "Hey! There's a balloon man!" Mae knew not to ask for a balloon. The Shermans could rarely afford extras and luxuries. "Why does it say 'three five zero' on the balloons?"

"That's three hundred and fifty," said Mrs. Sherman, "for Camden Falls's three hundred and fiftieth birthday."

Nikki let out a sigh of pleasure. She and Tobias and Mae and their mother had been in town since the parade had started. They had stood in the crowd and cheered when the Needle and Thread float glided by, and Nikki had been astonished to see a very uncomfortable-looking Flora dressed in a too-tight costume riding self-consciously with Ruby and Olivia and the others, trying to appear as if she knew how to operate a spinning wheel. After the parade, the Shermans had wandered to the town square, where Nikki had located Flora and a strangely quiet Olivia along with an equally quiet Annika Lindgren. Awkward introductions had been made, and Nikki had been about to ask Flora what was going on when Ms. Angelo, the director of the Camden Falls Children's Chorus, had raised her hands, and Ruby and the other members of the chorus had sung the first sweet strains of "This Land Is Your Land." They had followed with two other songs, and then Ms. Angelo had asked everyone to join the chorus in singing "Happy Birthday" to Camden Falls. Nikki and her mother and Tobias had sung softly, as they had the few times they'd been to church, but Mae had bellowed out the song, causing people standing near the Shermans to turn and smile.

Now it was noon. The Children's Chorus had drifted away, and Ruby, accompanied by Min, had left for CFE to get ready for the opening performance of *The Witches of Camden Falls*. The Shermans planned to spend most of the day in town. The judging of the exhibits would take place in the afternoon, and Nikki's mother had promised that all the Shermans would be on hand at the Fongs' studio when prizes were awarded for the drawings and paintings.

"I'm hungry," announced Mae.

"Then let's get lunch," said Mrs. Sherman. "What do you want? There's Bud's cart."

"Could we go to the food stalls?" asked Nikki, pointing down Main Street. "I see signs for hamburgers and corn on the cob and strawberry shortcake and all kinds of things."

"I see someone selling cotton candy!" cried Mae. "Could I have cotton candy?"

"Not for lunch," replied her mother. "Maybe for dessert."

"Really?" said Mae. "This is too exciting!" She let go of Nikki's and Tobias's hands and skipped around her mother.

The Shermans made their way through the crowd on Main Street, passing people dressed in colonial costumes, a woman selling penny candy, a German shepherd wearing a tricorn hat, and a man giving rides in a horse-drawn buggy. Nikki peered into several stores. As they passed Needle and Thread, she saw the displays of quilts and felt her stomach jump as she thought of the exhibit at the Fongs', her three carefully chosen drawings hanging somewhere on the walls.

When the Shermans reached the food stalls, Nikki's mother opened her wallet, counted the bills, thought for a moment, then handed several dollars to each of her children. "You choose what you want," she said.

Nikki took Mae by the hand again, and they looked at every one of the stalls before making their decisions. In the end, Nikki bought corn on the cob, a barbecued rib, and something called a funnel cake. Mae ate a hot dog in a great hurry and then begged to look for the cotton candy man again.

Half an hour later, their stomachs full, the Shermans met in front of Time and Again, and Mrs. Sherman said, "Should we check out the exhibits now? Tell me what's going on, Nikki."

"Well, the art exhibit is at the Fongs' studio. Let's not go there until later, when the prizes are awarded, okay?"

"Okay," said Mrs. Sherman.

"Then there's the photography exhibit. That's at the community center, and Olivia entered some of her pictures. The history exhibit is at the library, and Flora entered her book. Did I tell you she wrote a book?"

"An actual book?" said Mrs. Sherman.

Nikki nodded. "Yup. She had it bound and everything." She paused, thinking. "Oh, and there's a display of quilts at Needle and Thread — actually, two displays."

"How do you know all this, little sister?" asked Tobias.

Nikki shrugged, smiling. She had lived in Camden Falls all her life, but she hadn't truly felt a part of the town until she had become friends with Flora and Ruby and Olivia. And, she had to admit, until her father had left and the Shermans had allowed themselves to emerge from their isolated world in the country. "I just do," she told her brother.

"Where should we start?" he asked.

"With the photos, I think," said Nikki. "Then we'll go to the library, and then to Needle and Thread."

The community center was crowded, but its doors stood invitingly open, and a woman wearing a long dress and a wig of brown curls ushered the Shermans inside and pointed out a stack of brochures. Nikki picked one up, saw that it was an alphabetical arrangement of the photographers' names, turned to the back, and found the listing for *Walter, Olivia*.

"'Ten years old. Wildlife photos,'" Nikki read. "'Numbers sixty-one through sixty-three.'"

For twenty minutes, the Shermans wandered through the community center, examining photos of Camden Falls people and Camden Falls buildings and Camden Falls streets and Camden Falls festivals. At last, they came to a wall labeled CAMDEN FALLS WILDLIFE.

"Olivia thought she was going to photograph every kind of animal and insect and bird that lives here," Nikki told her family. "She was surprised when she found out she could only enter three photos."

"Relieved, too, I'll bet," said Tobias.

Nikki looked at the photos Olivia had selected — a

very nice shot of a squirrel in the Walters' backyard, a picture of a cardinal that Nikki knew had been taken in Mr. Pennington's garden, and a shot of what looked like a puddle of water.

"What's this last picture supposed to be of?" asked Tobias.

"That's Olivia's art photo. It's a fish in that pond near school."

"Where's the fish?" asked Mae.

Nikki squinted. "There, I think. Olivia mostly liked the way the ripples in the water were shimmering."

The Shermans walked to the library next and were very impressed with Flora's book. "She interviewed all these old people," said Nikki, "and wrote down their stories." Nikki told her family about Flora's great-grandfather.

Tobias picked up the book and paged through it. "Wow. This is kind of amazing."

"I know," said Nikki. "And it turns out that the lives of most of these people are connected."

Mrs. Sherman took the book from Tobias. "Flora interviewed Mrs. Fitzpatrick? She's Mrs. DuVane's mother, you know."

Nikki nodded. "And Mrs. Fitzpatrick knew Mr. Pennington's father and she knows Mary Woolsey, and —"

"I'm bored," said Mae loudly.

"Let's go look at the quilts, then," said Nikki. "And after that, let's stop by the Fongs' to see when the judging will take place."

By the time the Shermans reached the studio, Mae had begun to whine.

"But look," said Nikki. "Look over there, Mae. Those are my drawings."

Nikki, her heart beginning to pound, crossed the polished floor of the Fongs' studio. For a moment, she felt as if everyone else in the room had somehow slid away and she was alone, being pulled toward the wall where her drawings, now matted, hung beside small signs reading NICOLETTE SHERMAN, AGE TWELVE. Two of the drawings were of Paw-Paw, the third was a study of a snakeskin. She knew that some people found snakes revolting, but she had thought the skin, with its intricate pattern, was beautiful, and she had drawn it in careful detail.

"Very impressive, sis," said Tobias, reaching her side.

Nikki couldn't respond. She had never seen her work look so professional.

"Honey, this is wonderful," said her mother. "I'm awfully proud of you."

After a moment, Nikki said quietly, "I see Mr. Fong. I'm going to ask him what time the judging's supposed to take place."

"Four o'clock," was his reply.

Nikki looked at Mae, who was sitting on her mother's knee, saying, "But I'm hungry. And I'm thirsty. And I'm tired of walking around." (She dragged out "around" until it had three syllables.)

"Mom, if you want to take Mae home, that's okay," said Nikki, a wave of disappointment washing over her.

"Nonsense. I wouldn't dream of it. I'll take Mae back to the community center for a while. They're going to be showing children's films there all afternoon. Mae just needs a rest. We'll meet you and Tobias here at four."

Nikki breathed a sigh of relief. "Thank you," she said.

Tobias left then to find friends, and Nikki returned to the library, where she hoped to meet up with Olivia and Flora. She was pleased to find them there, along with Annika. But she was dismayed when she saw that none of them was smiling.

"What's wrong?" asked Nikki.

"The photos and the history projects have already been judged," Flora replied.

"Oh. And . . . you didn't win anything? I'm really sorry," said Nikki, feeling her stomach go hollow as she realized that that probably meant none of her drawings would win a prize, either.

"No," said Flora. "I got second place in the elementary division."

"And I got an honorable mention," said Olivia.

"But that's wonderful!" exclaimed Nikki. "Why aren't you celebrating or something?"

"It's hard to explain," said Flora.

"Yeah," agreed Olivia.

"You know what? Sometimes you guys are weird," said Nikki.

At exactly four o'clock that afternoon, Nikki stood with her mother, Tobias, Mae, and a crowd of people, including Flora, Olivia, and Annika, in the Fongs' studio. A smiling Mr. Fong, holding a fistful of ribbons, had just announced, "I am pleased to award prizes to the top entries in five categories." He went on to describe the categories (Nikki wasn't paying attention — her head was swimming and she slipped her hand into her mother's) and then said, "My wife and I looked through stacks and stacks of amazing artwork, and we had a hard time making a decision, but in the end, we were able to choose a first place, a second place, a third place, and four honorable mentions in each category. Here's the list of winners."

Nikki gripped her mother's hand tightly when Mr. Fong reached the elementary category. He announced the honorable mentions first, then third place, and then second. Nikki's name had not been read. She let go of her mother's hand and tried to hold back the tears that were burning her eyes. And then Mr. Fong said,

"Finally, first place goes to Nicolette Sherman for her study of a snakeskin."

Nikki grabbed her mother's hand again and felt the tears — happy ones — begin to fall. Her friends whooped and cheered. Mae jumped up and down. Mrs. Sherman hugged Nikki, and Tobias leaned down to whisper to her, "You see what Shermans can do? Anything at all. What does Dad know?"

That night, even though she could barely afford it, Mrs. Sherman took her entire family out to dinner in Camden Falls, the first time in Sherman family history.

# CHAPTER 17

# *Starring Ruby J. Northrop*

On Saturday morning, some butterflies took up residence in Ruby's stomach and seemed to increase in number as the day wore on. Ruby could feel them as she rode on the Needle and Thread float in the parade, just a little flutter of wings here and there. She could feel them as she stood in the town square with the rest of the Children's Chorus and sang "This Land Is Your Land." (The fluttering had increased to flapping.) And during the rest of the day, after Min dropped her at Camden Falls Elementary, the butterflies increased their vigor. By the time Ruby was in her costume and had had her makeup applied (sitting meekly in the hallway between Ms. Holton's room and Mr. Levithan's room), the butterflies, herds of them, seemed to be tap-dancing in her stomach.

"Are you all right, Ruby?" asked Mrs. Gillipetti. "You look a little pale."

"I'm okay," she replied. (Tap, tap, tappety-tap.)

"You're sure? You aren't sick, are you?"

"Just nervous, I guess."

"All right," said Mrs. Gillipetti uncertainly.

Ruby wished with all her heart that Aunt Allie hadn't moved back to Camden Falls. Then she wished that Aunt Allie wasn't her aunt. Then she wished, somewhat more reasonably, that Aunt Allie wasn't going to be sitting in the audience that night.

Aunt Allie had ruined everything.

Ruby had spent the last few weeks concentrating so hard on being able to show her aunt what a wonderful and professional actress she was — one with true potential for stardom — that she had enjoyed very little of the hours and hours of rehearsal time.

Darn old Aunt Allie, thought Ruby miserably as she sat apart from everyone in the corridor outside the auditorium. She had assumed one of her yoga positions and had tried to clear her mind, but every time it was just about empty, an image of Aunt Allie would intrude in a most annoying fashion. Ruby could hear her saying, "You have no dressing room. You're performing in an elementary school. This is just a school play. . . ." And then the butterflies beat their wings harder than ever.

"Ruby?" A voice called to her from down the hall-way. Ruby turned and saw Min. "All ready, honey?"

"I guess."

"The auditorium is really filling up. Flora and Aunt Allie are in their seats. All your friends are here, too. . . . Are you okay?"

"Why does everybody keep asking me that?" cried Ruby.

Min looked around at the rest of the cast, most of whom were running noisily through the corridors, laughing and calling and chattering. "You just seem a little . . . I don't know. Are you" — Min chose her words carefully — "are you sad because your parents can't be here for your big night?"

Well, now I am, thought Ruby.

"Five minutes to curtain call!" announced Mrs. Gillipetti then, and Min gave Ruby a hug.

"Remember," said Min, "we're all here for you. Break a leg! I know you're going to be a hit." Min hurried back to the auditorium.

Ruby concentrated on breathing deeply.

"One minute to curtain call," said Mrs. Gillipetti. "Ruby, are you *positive* you're all right?"

"Yes!"

Ruby took her place backstage. The curtain was down, the stage was dark, and Ruby could hear a great din from the other side of the curtain. Moments later, the first notes of the piano and violin sounded, played by the Central High students who made up the small orchestra.

The curtain rose.

The stage was slowly lit.

And Ruby J. Northrop stood before what felt like all of Camden Falls, Massachusetts.

For one horrifying moment, she couldn't remember what was supposed to happen next. Then her line came to her and she spoke it clearly, and just loudly enough.

But not with any emotion, thought Ruby, panicking.

Someone in the audience coughed. Someone else sneezed.

The cardboard tree standing next to John Parson's house began to teeter. Ever so subtly, Ruby reached out and steadied it. The teetering tree had been quite amateurish, Ruby knew, but her response to the problem had been professional. She hoped Aunt Allie had noticed. Ruby was pleased with herself, and some of the butterflies lost their energy.

The play continued. Ruby concentrated on her lines. The first scene came to an end. The second scene came to an end. The third scene began and Ruby willed herself to think of nothing but the story that she and the cast were telling. She placed herself hundreds of years back in time, in the life of the beleaguered Alice

Kendall, and suddenly found that she *was* Alice. When Harry Lang accused her, rather more sharply than usual, of being a witch, her tears came easily and naturally. They slid down her cheeks, and she allowed them to fall without wiping at them, knowing that not calling attention to them actually called quite a bit of attention to them and made her performance remarkable indeed.

The audience was hushed, but at the end of the scene, burst into spontaneous applause.

And with that, Ruby's butterflies disappeared entirely. She was, at last, able to enjoy her role.

Ruby glided through the rest of the performance and felt quite proud of it, even though later one of the kindergartners wandered onto the stage when it wasn't her scene. Ruby thought quickly and ad-libbed a line: "Run along now, duck, and find your mother." (She liked the addition of the old-fashioned-sounding "duck.") Then she shooed the girl into the wings. Toward the end of the play, shortly before Ruby's long-awaited death scene, Harry said, "So let this be a lesson to you, Ruby," and stood smirking, waiting for Ruby's reply. The audience caught his mistake and Ruby heard a few snickers. Again she thought quickly, and after the briefest of moments, said, "I know of no one in these parts who goeth by the name of Ruby, so assuredly you meant to calleth me by my given name of Alice."

"Uh, yeah," said Harry.

Ruby picked up with her next line, aware of laughter but pleased with herself, and then launched into Alice's best-ever death scene. Shortly after that, the curtain came down on colonial Camden Falls, and the auditorium erupted in cheering and applause.

I did it! thought Ruby. She looked at Mrs. Gillipetti, who was standing in the wings, wearing a broad smile.

"Wonderful," said Mrs. Gillipetti quietly. "Just wonderful, everybody. Okay. Get ready for the curtain call."

Later, Ruby found that although she could recall the first scenes of the play quite clearly, much of it, including the curtain call, had become a blur to her. She remembered lots and lots of clapping and even some whistling and cheering. She vaguely remembered seeing the smallest children run onto the stage holding hands, so that when one of them tripped, the entire row fell down. She remembered watching Harry walk onto the stage alone, watched him grinning and waving at the audience. And she definitely remembered what happened when she walked onto the stage herself. The audience, which had been noisy, fell silent. The clapping stopped. The cheering stopped. The whistling stopped. Then each person in the audience stood, raised his arms, and clasped his hands above his head, forming a lopsided circle.

Ruby, confused, looked at the rows of ringed arms,

and Mrs. Gillipetti leaned over and whispered, "They're giving you a standing O."

The audience had just taken their seats again when a stream of people, each holding a bouquet of flowers, walked down the aisle and approached the stage. One by one, they stepped onto the stage and presented a member of the cast or crew with a bouquet. Some received more than one.

Olivia handed Ruby a small bouquet and whispered, "This is from Nikki and Flora and me."

Min placed a bouquet of roses in her arms and said, "This is from Aunt Allie and me, and from your parents, too, because I know they're here tonight."

Ruby felt tears spring to her eyes, and she pulled Min to her in a tight hug.

Bouquet after bouquet was delivered. Mrs. Gillipetti received three, each member of the orchestra received one, and the lighting director received one.

Ruby was in a happy muddle of tears, chatter, and flowers, the cast members giving one another high fives, when a tall woman wearing what Min would call a no-nonsense suit strode onto the stage. Once again, the auditorium fell silent.

"Ladies and gentlemen," said Mrs. Gillipetti, "a few words from Mayor Howie."

Ruby turned to Harry and mouthed, "The *mayor*?"

Harry nodded, eyebrows raised.

"This," began Mayor Howie, "has been a wonderful event. Everyone involved in the production should be very, very proud. What you've seen here tonight," she said to the audience, "represents months of hard work, dedication, and ingenuity. Kudos to the cast and crew of *The Witches of Camden Falls*."

Ruby watched the mayor stride off the stage. She decided that if, when she was grown up, she didn't get to be an actor for some reason, then she definitely wanted to be a mayor.

Mrs. Gillipetti now took Mayor Howie's spot on the stage, raised her hands, and said above the din, "Thank you all for coming and for your support. Remember that our final performance will take place tomorrow afternoon at two o'clock. Spread the word."

Ruby was following Harry into the wings, feeling sad that opening night was over, when she felt someone take her by the elbow.

"Ruby Northrop?" asked a man's voice.

"Yes?" Ruby turned around.

"Douglas Geoffries," he said, holding out his hand. "I'm with the *Camden Falls Courier*. Could I have a few words with you?"

"Sure!" said Ruby, who then answered Mr. Geoffries's questions about her age and how long she'd been living in Camden Falls and other performances she'd been in.

The paper was published on the following Wednesday. When a copy was slapped down on the front doorstep of the fourth Row House from the left, Ruby snapped it up, turned the pages until she found the article about *The Witches of Camden Falls,* and scanned it for her interview. There was her name in print. And there was a photo of her and Harry onstage. Ruby cut out the article and tacked it to her bulletin board. She was very proud of it. It made her feel as happy as when Aunt Allie, on the drive home after opening night, had reached into the backseat of Min's car, taken Ruby by the hand, and said, "You were wonderful, dear."

# CHAPTER 18

# *Best Friends*

It was a silent group of girls who gathered at the fairgrounds outside Camden Falls on Sunday morning. Flora and Annika had said little to each other the previous evening, but they'd been at Ruby's performance, so they hadn't had much opportunity to talk. When Mrs. Walter brought her car around to the front of the Row Houses on Sunday and tooted the horn, Flora and Annika had walked slowly outside and slid into the Walters' car, where they had found a very quiet Olivia. Barely a word was spoken on the drive to the fairgrounds.

"Everything okay, girls?" Mrs. Walter asked later as they were climbing out of the car.

"Yeah," said Olivia.

"Yup," said Flora.

"Mm-hmm," said Annika.

"You're sure?"

"Yes!" said Olivia.

"Well, all right. I'll see you later. Olivia, your dad's working at the store today, but I'll bring Henry and Jack here at noon. Look for us at the information booth. I'll want to check in with you then, okay?"

"Okay."

The girls approached the entrance to the fair. Nikki was waiting for them. "Hi," she said.

"Hi," said Flora, Olivia, and Annika.

After a long and very uncomfortable silence, Flora finally said, "What should we do first?"

This was met with three shrugs.

"The midway?" suggested Flora.

A pause. Then, "I guess," said Olivia.

"Don't be so enthusiastic," said Annika.

"Look who's talking," said Olivia.

Nikki cleared her throat. "Does someone want to tell me what's going on? You guys were quiet all day yesterday. Are you mad at each other? Did you have a fight?"

"No," said Olivia, Flora, and Annika.

"Then what *is* it? Are you going to act like this all day? Because if you are, Mom and Mae are here, and I could have a lot more fun with them."

"So go find them," said Olivia.

"All right. Maybe I will." Nikki turned around.

"Wait, don't go," said Flora. "You know what, you guys? I think we need to talk."

"About what?" asked Annika sullenly.

"About us. Look. Annika, this is your first visit here. And Olivia, I think it's bothering you that Annika was my best friend before I moved to Camden Falls. And Annika, I think it's bothering you that Olivia and Nikki are my best friends now."

There was another pause, and then Nikki said, "And, Flora, I think it's bothering you that your friends aren't getting along."

"It is!" Flora exclaimed, and suddenly felt tears coming on. She swallowed a sob. "I love all of you. You *are* my friends. And I was looking forward to introducing Annika to you. And you to Annika. But this is" (Flora now let out a sob she couldn't control) "this is horrible."

Olivia put her arm around Flora. "I think we can work things out, though, don't you?"

"I hope so," said Flora.

"Well, if what you just said is true — that we're all friends and you love all of us — then I'm pretty sure we can."

Through her tears, Flora saw that Annika and Olivia were crying now, too. "This is so embarrassing! We can't all cry here in front of everybody," Flora exclaimed, eyeing the groups of people who kept hurrying toward the entrance to the fair.

"We need to go somewhere to talk," said Olivia, looking around. The fairgrounds, which on ordinary days were the town playing fields, consisted of a large grassy area surrounded on three sides by woods. Not far from where the girls stood was a graceful spruce tree, its sweeping branches spreading low. Olivia pointed to it. "Let's go sit under the tree. We can face the woods. That will be pretty private."

The girls walked shakily to the tree, sniffing and hiccupping, and now Nikki was wiping her eyes, too. "Are you sure we need to talk?" she asked. "That doesn't always work well at my house. I mean, it didn't when my father was around. No matter what anybody said, you couldn't win an argument with him. And then he and my mother would get madder than ever at each other and finally Dad would go crashing out of the house, yelling at all of us."

"Well, we're not your father," said Flora gently. "This talk isn't going to end that way."

The girls sat down in a circle behind the tree.

"I hope someone has Kleenex," said Annika, wiping her eyes.

"I do," said Olivia, reaching into her pocket with a trembling hand.

"All right. Let's start at the beginning," said Nikki.

"What's the beginning?" asked Flora. "I mean, what's the beginning of . . . this?"

Nikki said slowly, "I think the beginning was a couple of months ago when you told us that Annika was going to visit." She glanced at Olivia.

Olivia, her cheeks reddening, said to Nikki, "Yeah. I knew Annika was Flora's best friend before she moved here. And now *we're* best friends — I mean, you and Flora and Ruby and I are — but I was afraid that when Annika came, Flora would see what she was missing."

"What do you mean?" asked Flora.

Olivia shrugged.

"No, really. What do you mean?" asked Nikki. "This is important, Olivia. If we're going to talk about this stuff, then we'd better *really* talk about it. Because if we don't, we're going to create distances."

"I'm afraid that if we *do* talk we're going to create distances."

"Not if we're already friends," said Flora. "And we are."

Olivia drew her breath in and said, "I never had a best friend before. No one liked me, not really. I skipped a grade, and I'm smaller than everyone in our class, and I'm interested in things no one else cares about. So I never expected to have a best friend. Then I got three, but I was always afraid that everything could be taken away. Why should you guys like *me* so much? So when Flora said Annika was coming to visit and she talked about all the great things Annika used to do, I felt like I —" Olivia stopped talking suddenly.

"What?" asked Annika. "Like you what?"

"Like I wasn't going to measure up," whispered Olivia. "Like Flora would see Annika again and realize what she was missing."

"But I was afraid I wasn't going to measure up!" cried Annika. "Flora e-mails me about the great friends she has in Camden Falls and all the things you guys do together. So I guess I —" Now it was Annika's turn to stop talking.

"It's okay. You can tell us," said Olivia.

"Well, I was jealous of you and Nikki. I'm even a little jealous of Camden Falls."

"Of Camden Falls?" repeated Flora.

"Yeah. You're always going on about how wonderful it is here —"

"She is?" said Nikki.

"Yes. And, Flora, I want you to be happy and everything. I do. But — and I know this doesn't make sense — somehow I didn't want you to be happier here than you were — I mean, I didn't want you to forget — it's just that I didn't want to lose you." And with that, Annika burst into tears and buried her head in her hands.

Then Nikki started to cry.

"Why are *you* crying?" asked Olivia, bewildered.

"Because a year ago," said Nikki, sobbing, "I could never, ever have had this kind of talk with anyone. I didn't have any friends, either, Olivia, and now I have three best friends. You guys, think about why we're crying. It's actually because we have so *many* friends. Annika, Flora can be friends with us and with you. Olivia, Flora can be friends with Annika and with us. Right?"

"Right," said Annika and Olivia.

But now Flora began to weep. "You know why I was so upset when my project only won second place?" she said.

"I truly have no idea," said Nikki. "I've been wondering about it since yesterday."

"It was because I wanted Annika to see how happy I am here. I wanted her to see that I fit in. I thought if I could win first place with a project about Camden Falls and my family and everything, then I could *prove* that I fit in, and that I belong here."

Olivia started to laugh.

"It isn't funny, Olivia!" cried Flora.

"Well, this is: I wanted to win first place with my photos so I could impress Annika."

"Oh, for the love of Mike," said Flora, sounding so much like Min that Annika and Nikki began to laugh, too, and then finally so did Flora.

"You guys!" Annika exclaimed.

Olivia looked at her watch. "It's nearly eleven o'clock," she said. "We're missing the fair."

"And it's Annika's last day here," said Flora.

"Somehow I think our talk was more important," said Nikki. "We really needed to have it. Is everybody clear on everything?" she added. "Annika, I think Flora is always going to be your friend. You're not going to lose her. And, Flora, Annika sees that you're happy. Olivia, whether you like it or not, you have best friends for life."

"Same goes for you," said Olivia to Nikki.

Nikki stood up and brushed off her jeans. "Well, all right, then."

Olivia, Flora, and Annika stood, too, and the girls put their arms around one another and headed back to the entrance to the fair.

"We have four hours before we have to meet Min and Annika's parents," said Flora, "and then Annika will have to go home."

"What should we do first?" asked Nikki.

"Midway," said Olivia. "And I have to remember to check in with my mom."

"After that we'll get lunch," said Annika.

"Oh, look!" exclaimed Flora. "There's one of those photo booths. Let's see if we can all fit in it."

They could, just barely. And the strip of photos, when it was ready, showed most of Flora's head, the right side of Nikki's head, the left side of Olivia's head, and the top of Annika's head.

"Who's going to keep it?" asked Annika.

"We all will," said Flora. "I have an idea. Let me have it for now."

Flora had to wait until Tuesday, after she had said good-bye to Annika and her parents, after the second performance of Ruby's play, after another day at the fair (this time with Nikki and Olivia and Ruby), after an impressive fireworks display, and after school had begun again, before she could carry out her idea. Then she took the strip of photos to Camden Falls Art Supply, Xeroxed it three times, carefully cut out the strips of photos, and asked to have each strip laminated.

"There," she said that evening as she showed them to Min. "Four bookmarks. One for each of us to remember the fair by. I'll give Olivia and Nikki theirs tomorrow."

Flora put Annika's bookmark in an envelope and added a note that said *"Friends forever and always"* and mailed it to her the next day.

# CHAPTER 19

# The New Old House

Over and done in a flash.

That was how Ruby thought of Camden Falls's 350th birthday celebration. How, she wondered, was it possible to plan for something for so long, to prepare for it, to look forward to it, to dream about it — and then to find yourself on the other side of it so quickly? This was exactly what happened with her birthday every year. And with Christmas. And even with summer vacation, which lasted much longer than any of those other things but still managed to fly by, so that when it was over, Ruby found herself shaking her head in wonderment.

The celebration was truly over. The posters were gone. Store windows now advertised gas grills and inflatable swimming pools. The town decorations had been replaced with . . . "Nothing," said Ruby glumly.

**171**

With the exception of the pots of flowers, the decorations had simply been taken down and put away. And the Camden Falls Elementary auditorium was preparing for sixth-grade graduation. All signs of *The Witches of Camden Falls* had disappeared.

Over and done in a flash.

At least I have the newspaper article and the program from the play, thought Ruby. She looked at them frequently. She thought of them as her moment in the sun. When she mentioned this to Min, Min smiled and said, "I have a feeling you'll be having lots more moments in the sun, Ruby. You're only ten years old."

Ruby, who was thinking that she was *already* ten years old, said nothing and went into the backyard to sit on a lawn chair and reflect on her life.

She was ten. Fourth grade was almost over. In the fall, she would begin fifth grade. It had been a good year for Ruby, if you didn't count her report cards. Ruby's report cards were never the sort that made grown-ups smile and congratulate her. They were more the sort that made her teachers shake their heads and discuss her attitude and potential. But oh well. There had been the play, and riding on the Needle and Thread float in the parade, and several performances of the Camden Falls Children's Chorus, and talk of moving Ruby to the advanced tap class (the Turbo Tappers) at her dance school. Ruby decided she could be proud of her life so far. And Min was probably right. There would be many more moments in the sun.

The one thing that felt off-kilter to Ruby was Aunt Allie. Ruby decided that she and Aunt Allie were like C and C sharp on the piano. Individually they were fine, but put them together and they sounded like King Comma on his way to the vet. Ruby and her aunt had had some good moments, it was true. After all, Aunt Allie had congratulated Ruby on the opening night of *The Witches of Camden Falls* and sounded as if she meant what she'd said. But mostly they crabbed at each other.

And now — in just two weeks — Aunt Allie would be moving into her new house. So why didn't Ruby feel happy about this? Aunt Allie would be out of her hair. C sharp would be gone. But when Ruby thought about moving day, she felt a small sadness, which she now realized was due to the fact that she believed she had failed where her aunt was concerned. She and her aunt *ought* to be able to get along. They were family. And yet . . .

Ruby's head was beginning to ache. Still, she felt quite mature for coming to the conclusion that she, Ruby, contributed to the problems with Aunt Allie — much as Ruby would like to place all the blame on her aunt.

Flora joined Ruby at the lawn chair then. "Scootch up your feet," she said. "Let me sit on the end."

Ruby obliged. Then she yawned and said, "Feels like summer."

"Pretty soon it will be summer for real," said Flora. "Can you believe it? And then we will have been here for one entire year."

"I actually can't believe it," said Ruby. "It doesn't feel like a year."

"It feels like a year since Aunt Allie got here, though," said Flora.

"*Shh!*" hissed Ruby, giggling. "Her window's open."

"Oh, she's clacking away at that computer of hers. She'll never hear us."

"No she isn't," said Ruby. "I mean, she isn't writing. She's packing."

Flora was quiet for a moment. She reached down to stroke Daisy Dear, who had crawled under the lawn chair — even though she barely fit and her back was jammed up against Ruby's bottom. "What are you doing there, Daisy?" she asked.

"Daisy wilts in the heat. She's a shade seeker," said Ruby wisely.

"I like Aunt Allie's new house, don't you?"

Ruby nodded. "Her new old house."

"I guess it is her new old house," replied Flora, smiling.

The house Allie bought had been built in 1897.

"I wonder if it has any ghosts," said Ruby.

"Oh, no. Don't say that!" cried Flora. "I'll think of it every time we go over there."

"Which hopefully won't be very often."

"Anyway, the Row Houses are older than Aunt Allie's house, and we don't have any ghosts."

"That we know of," said Ruby.

Flora shivered.

The next two weeks were busy ones for Aunt Allie. She called the phone company. She called the electric company. She changed her address. She traveled to New York City to supervise the packing of the remainder of the things in her old apartment. She cleaned the new house, finished packing up the things in her room at the Row House, then cleaned the room. To Allie's surprise, Ruby offered to help with the last two of these chores.

"I'm a good packer and a good cleaner," she announced. "And if you want me to do things a certain way, I'm good at following directions." This was not quite true. Ruby was only good at following directions onstage, but why split hairs?

"Well . . . thank you," said Aunt Allie. "I could use a little help. Why don't you start by packing up the books? You can put them in those cartons that are under the window. Just don't fill them too full or we'll never be able to lift them."

"Aren't the movers going to carry them?" asked Ruby.

"Yes, but we have to get them downstairs first. The movers are going to start out in Manhattan and then drive up here. I told them we'd have these things waiting by the front door."

So Ruby packed books and wrapped breakable things in newspaper and dusted shelves and tried not to appear too crabby when Aunt Allie asked her if she was certain she shouldn't be doing her homework instead.

"Why don't you help, too?" Ruby asked Flora on the evening before the big move.

Flora, who was sitting at her desk, working on a report about the wives of the presidents, replied by saying, "Isn't it weird that there are no husbands of presidents? That doesn't seem quite right."

"Flora?" said Ruby.

"What?"

"I said, why don't you help Aunt Allie, too? If you did, it would be good karma. Besides, it's Friday night. You have all weekend to finish your homework."

"I don't like moving," said Flora flatly.

Ruby stepped all the way into Flora's room. "But you'd be speeding Aunt Allie on her way."

"Ruby!" Flora spun around in her desk chair. "I want her gone as much as you do," she said in a loud whisper, "but I don't like packing and vans and cartons and everything. It reminds me of — oh, never mind."

"What? You can't not tell me," said Ruby.

"It reminds me of when we moved here, okay?" said Flora. "And that was not my best time. I'm happy to be here, but moving makes me think of Mom and Dad and all the stuff we left behind. So stop talking about it."

Ruby backed out of the room.

On Saturday, Ruby said to her sister, "Are you going to be okay today?"

"I guess. I'll just be happy when it's all over. When the room upstairs is back to normal and when Aunt Allie's house is set up. What time are the movers supposed to get here?"

"Right after lunch, I think."

The movers arrived at one-thirty. They added the boxes stacked in the front hall of the Row House to the van and then followed Aunt Allie (proudly driving her new Subaru) through Camden Falls to her home. Min, Flora, and Ruby followed the van in Min's car. The van backed into Allie's driveway, and Allie and Min parked on the street in front of the house.

Ruby and Flora emerged from the car to find their aunt in tears on her front porch.

"What's the matter?" they asked. Ruby wondered why on earth adults had to cry. It was so unsettling. Why couldn't they leave the crying to kids?

"Oh," said Aunt Allie, searching her purse for Kleenex, "this is just silliness. It's a happy day. But I can't believe I've left New York for good. I lived there for so long, and I considered myself a city person, and now here I am back in a small town."

"But I thought this is what you wanted," said Ruby.

"It is."

"Oh." Aunt Allie, Ruby thought, was not only C sharp, she was also a big knot of yarn that you couldn't untangle. Even if you found one of the ends and pulled on it, the rest of the yarn would just bunch up more tightly.

Aunt Allie wiped at her eyes, put the Kleenex back in her pocket, and said, "Girls, there's something I want to show you, and I think now is as good a time as any. Come upstairs with me."

Ruby and Flora followed Aunt Allie through the front door of her house, into the empty first floor, and then up the stairs to the second floor. At the top of the stairs, Allie stepped aside and said, "Go to the room at the end of the hall."

Ruby glanced at her sister, then walked down the hall, her footsteps echoing softly. The door to the room was closed. "Go ahead. Open it," Ruby heard Allie say.

Ruby opened the door and found a room that was already furnished, right down to the knickknacks. "It's beautiful!" exclaimed Ruby softly. She and Flora stepped inside and admired the twin beds, each covered with a purple chenille spread and awash in brightly colored pillows. Between the beds was a white bookcase, filled with books. One wall of the room had been painted with a scene from Paris. On a dresser sat china figurines and framed photos of Min and Aunt Allie and Flora and Ruby's parents, and even Olivia and Nikki.

"Whose room is it?" asked Flora in a whisper.

"Yours," said Aunt Allie. "Yours and Ruby's. I made sure it was ready first. It's yours for whenever you want to visit. Okay?"

"Okay," said Flora.

"Thank you," said Ruby.

Ruby was envisioning dinners of tofu and kale at Aunt Allie's, and evenings spent completing crossword puzzles and homework assignments. Still, she gave her aunt an awkward hug, joined by Flora.

"This was a very good surprise," said Ruby solemnly.

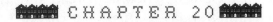

# CHAPTER 20

# Congratulations!

June was the month of graduations. Robby Edwards graduated from the high school proudly with his certificate of attendance. Tobias Sherman graduated from the high school proudly but with no clear idea of what he wanted to do next. A week later, Flora, Nikki, and Olivia graduated from Camden Falls Elementary. A day after that, Alyssa Morris graduated from preschool.

"I haven't seen so many caps and gowns since your aunt Allie graduated from college," said Min.

Of all the graduates, Robby was perhaps the most excited. "It means I can start my job," he said. "It means no more school for babies. It means I'm a man." And then he asked his mother for the sixth or seventh time, "Are you *sure* our class gets to graduate with the rest of the high school kids? We won't have to graduate with the babies at the elementary school, will we?"

"No," said his mother patiently. "Your teacher promised. The only reason your class was moved to CFE was because of space. You'll graduate with the twelfth-graders. And, Robby, remember that Flora and Ruby and Olivia will be graduating from CFE, and I'm sure they don't think of themselves as babies. Okay?"

"Okay," said Robby. "Oh, I hope it doesn't rain! I really hope it doesn't rain! We need sunshine for high school graduation! I better wish on a star. That usually works."

Robby's wish came partially true. Graduation day was overcast and dreary but no rain fell. The ceremony was held at four o'clock on a June Thursday in the Camden Falls Central High School football stadium. As there was open attendance, the bleachers were packed.

Olivia had begged to go. She'd known Robby all her life. "Please, please, please?" she'd said to her father the week before graduation.

"But your mother and I will be working at the store."

"I could go with Min. She's taking Flora and Ruby."

"All right," said Mr. Walter. "You can go. And why don't you put together a Congratulations basket for Robby?"

"What do you suppose people wear to graduations?" Olivia asked Flora on the phone on Wednesday
night.

"I don't know, but I think you're supposed to look
pretty nice."

"Should we wear dresses?"

"Maybe."

"I'll ask Nikki what she's going to wear." Olivia
hung up the phone and dialed Nikki's number. "Hi,"
she said. "Guess what. Flora and Ruby and I are going
to the graduation, too."

"Oh, to see Robby," said Nikki.

"And Tobias. Anyway, we wanted to know what
you're going to wear."

"Uh-oh. I didn't even think about that. You know
what I *have* been thinking about?"

"What?"

"What if my father gets to feeling guilty and decides
he should come back to see Tobias graduate?"

Olivia felt a chill wash over her. She remembered
what had happened when Mr. Sherman had returned
after Christmas. "You don't think he would, though,
do you? I mean *why* would he come back, after what
Tobias did to him?"

"That's true," said Nikki slowly. "Still . . . Tobias is
his son."

"Well, let's not think about that. Let's think about our outfits," said Olivia.

In the end, Olivia, Nikki, Ruby, and Flora all decided to wear dresses. Flora's was one she had made herself, Ruby's was one she had worn in a dance recital (it was the fanciest of the four dresses, involving sequins, but Min couldn't talk her out of it), Olivia's was the one she wore when she went to church sometimes with her grandparents, and Nikki's was a brand-new one recently provided by Mrs. DuVane (who would also be attending the graduation). Nikki was supremely grateful for it.

"Isn't this exciting?" said Olivia as she and Flora and Ruby and Min walked across the high school lawn toward the stadium on Thursday.

"Look at all the caps and gowns," said Ruby. "It's like a flock of penguins."

"Penguins don't wear hats," said Olivia.

"Well, if they did," said Ruby.

"I wonder which one is Robby," said Flora.

"I wonder which one is Tobias," said Olivia.

"Come on, girls," said Min. "Let's find seats."

Flora and Ruby helped their grandmother navigate the steps of the bleachers until they reached a row with space for four people.

"Lord love a duck," said Min, puffing, as she sat down.

Olivia leafed through the program that had been handed to her as they approached the bleachers. She found Robby's name, then Tobias's. "I wonder where Nikki is sitting," she said aloud. "She was afraid her father might decide to show up."

"Lord love a duck," murmured Min again.

"But I'm sure he won't," added Olivia.

The members of the high school band, minus the graduating seniors, filed onto the football field then and sat in rows of chairs that had been arranged next to a podium. And then the seniors, all 322 of them, walked onto the field and sat in another, much bigger arrangement of chairs.

Olivia felt a flutter of excitement, but it faded quickly when a woman, who turned out to be the superintendent of the schools, stepped up to the podium and started to make a speech. A long speech. Olivia lost track of it early on and was relieved when the woman finally stopped talking. Unfortunately, when she finished, the high school principal made an even longer and duller speech. Luckily, this was followed by a speech given by the valedictorian of the graduating class, a girl who looked so much like Olivia that Olivia began to picture herself standing in front of that podium in six years. Now *that* was something to strive for. Valedictorian of her class.

At long last, the speeches were over and it was time to award the diplomas. They were to be handed out alphabetically by last name. Olivia looked for Robby. Then she looked for Tobias. And then she began to scan the stands for Mr. Sherman. She was startled when she felt Ruby nudge her and hiss, "Olivia, Robby's next!"

Olivia jumped to attention. She returned her gaze to the seniors. A boy named Nathaniel Edmond was shaking the hand of the superintendent and receiving his diploma. At the head of the line of waiting seniors was Robby. He was standing stiffly, arms at his sides, staring at Nathaniel and the superintendent.

Nathaniel walked back to his seat.

"Robert William Edwards!" called the superintendent.

A cheer arose from among the other seniors. In the stands around Olivia, people applauded and stamped their feet. Robby, grinning widely and waving at his audience, walked smartly to the podium. When he was handed his certificate of attendance, he shook hands, said thank you, and returned to his seat, tossing his cap in the air.

Tobias, when he accepted his diploma later, was more subdued, but as he left the podium, Min, Flora, Olivia, Ruby, Nikki, Mae, Mrs. DuVane, and Mrs. Sherman cheered loudly, and Ruby (feeling bad because Tobias's cheering section hadn't been as large as Robby's) inserted her fingers in her mouth and let out a piercing whistle, which caused Min to raise her eyebrows.

When the last diploma had been handed out, everyone left their seats and the football field was filled with excited seniors and equally excited families. Olivia decided that she had never seen so many cameras. Everywhere she looked were groups of people posing for someone's camera. Three girls in their caps and gowns threw their arms around one another and, nearly tumbling over sideways, grinned while a mom snapped their photo. Robby posed with his beloved Mrs. Fulton. A boy posed with his parents. The valedictorian posed with the principal.

"Gosh, just think," said Olivia wistfully, "this will be us next week."

And so it was. The week between was busy. Robby had his long-awaited graduation party and then began training to work at Sincerely Yours. Olivia and her friends finished up final assignments and cleaned out their desks. Olivia said a lot of good-byes (in her head). She said good-bye to the CFE playground and cafeteria and library. She said good-bye to her desk and the classroom she had so happily shared with Flora and Nikki. She bid good riddance to the gym, but even as she did so, she thought with a shudder of the even bigger and scarier gym she was likely to find at the high school.

On the afternoon of graduation day, Mr.

Donaldson sat on the edge of his desk and addressed Olivia's class, his first at CFE.

"You've been great," he said. "Memorable. My other classes are going to have a lot to live up to."

Olivia's classmates smiled, but Olivia could feel her lip trembling.

"All right," Mr. Donaldson continued. "I think you know what will go on this afternoon. Are there any questions, though? No? Okay. Be sure to arrive by four o'clock. And remember, white outfits for the girls — pants are fine — and white shirts and black pants for the guys, okay? See you in an hour or so."

Olivia slid out of her seat. She had cleaned out her desk along with everyone else, but now she stuck her hand inside to make sure she hadn't missed anything. She was hoping to find an old note from Nikki or an early assignment with Mrs. Mandel's handwriting at the top. But her desk was truly empty.

Olivia sighed.

Then she caught up with Flora and Ruby, called "See you later!" to Nikki, and headed for the Row Houses.

"Only two walks left," said Olivia as the girls turned onto Aiken Avenue, "not including this one."

"What?" said Ruby.

"Only two more walks to or from school."

"I'm sure you'll be back at CFE again sometime," said Ruby. "What about my graduation?"

"That won't be the same," said Olivia. "I mean two more walks when I'm a student here."

"Well, what about this: only one more disgusting school lunch tomorrow," said Ruby.

"I didn't even mind the lunches," replied Olivia.

"I wonder why you have to come back for one more day after you graduate," said Ruby.

"I don't know, but I'm glad we do." Olivia kicked at a pebble.

"Olivia, you're not going to be sad all afternoon, are you?" asked Flora. "Because this is supposed to be a happy occasion."

"Lots of happy occasions are sad, too," said Olivia.

"Actors love roles with complicated emotions," Ruby spoke up.

Olivia sighed again. "Well, my emotions certainly feel complicated today. Maybe it isn't the same for you. You guys have only been going to CFE for a year."

"But we had gone to our old school since pre-K," said Flora. "We miss our old school. We were sad to leave it."

"Sorry," said Olivia. "I wasn't thinking."

"It's all right," replied Flora, "but, Olivia, try to be happy about today, okay? We're only going to graduate from sixth grade once. We'd better enjoy it. Plus, afterward, we'll go to the party at your store. That will be fun, won't it?"

"Yes," said Olivia.

An hour later, Olivia and her parents and brothers pulled into the parking lot of CFE. The lot was packed.

"Honey, you're beautiful," Olivia's father said as they walked toward the school.

"Thank you," replied Olivia. She looked down at her dress, which Gigi had made just for this occasion and was the most grown-up dress Olivia had ever worn.

Later, sitting on her folding chair on the stage in the auditorium, Nikki a row in front of her, Flora a row in front of Nikki, Olivia tried hard to feel happy — to feel proud of her accomplishments and brave about the next school year. And she was certainly surprised and pleased when she was presented with the overall achievement award and thrilled with the cheering and applause that arose from the audience and her class-mates as she accepted her plaque. But as she returned to her seat and gazed around the auditorium at all its familiar details — the drooping hem of the curtain at the third window from the back, the chair in the front row that was missing its seat, the ceiling tiles, the new green carpeting — Olivia couldn't help but feel that a wonderful chapter in a book had come suddenly to its end.

The party at Sincerely Yours was all that Olivia could have hoped for. It reminded her, in fact, of her surprise one-oh birthday bash. Many of the same guests were there, and they were, Olivia realized, all the people who were the most important to her: her parents and her brothers, Gigi and Poppy, her aunt and uncle and cousins, her best friends, and her Row House neighbors.

She looked at the door to Sincerely Yours and saw the OPEN sign, which meant that people outside on Main Street saw the CLOSED sign. She looked at the CONGRATULATIONS, GRADUATES! banner draped along one wall. She watched Robby, who was telling every single person at the party, individually, that he would soon be an official employee of Sincerely Yours. She smiled at Mr. Pennington, who was sitting in a chair with baby Grace in his lap. She laughed when Ruby approached her wearing a cone-shaped party hat on her forehead as if she were a unicorn. She posed for a photo with Nikki and Flora, the three of them holding their diplomas and grinning.

And all the while, Olivia was thinking of this chapter in her life, the one that was ending, and realizing that she did not want to turn the page to see what would come next. She wished instead that she could go back to page one.

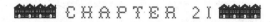 

# CHAPTER 21

# Summertime

This is Camden Falls, Massachusetts, on the first day of summer. The weather is warm and sultry, and in the afternoon, storm clouds will gather and the wind will pick up and thunder will roll, sending Min Read's dog, Daisy Dear, under the nearest bed. But for now, the sky is clear and there is no wind to rustle leaves or rattle doors.

It is ten o'clock in the morning, and Camden Falls is a busy place. Come look at Main Street. Here is Sincerely Yours, the newest store in town. In the kitchen, Mrs. Walter is stirring the mixture that will coat a batch of candy apples. In the front of the store, Mr. Walter is working the cash register, and Robby Edwards, wearing his new Sincerely Yours T-shirt, is helping a customer put together a birthday basket.

Down the block at Needle and Thread, Flora Northrop, who has now lived in Camden Falls for an entire year, is helping a class of eight-year-olds make felt change purses in the shape of turtles. Olivia Walter is on a couch, reading a book about ecosystems. Ruby Northrop is not at the store because she's playing at her friend Lacey's house.

If you are a visitor to Camden Falls, these might seem like small things and Camden Falls a very ordinary place. But everywhere extraordinary things are happening, if you know what to look for. For instance, next to Plaza Drugs another new store will soon open: The Marquis Diner. A family named Nelson has moved here from Boston to make a new life for themselves in a small town. Now step into Time and Again and see the man, the one in the wheelchair, working at the information desk. That's Sonny Sutphin, and this is the first job he has held in a very long time. Most people in town were surprised to find out how much about books and literature Sonny knew — enough to be given this particular job. For Sonny, having a job to go to every day is momentous. He feels as though he has spent the last few decades underwater, but now he is rising and rising toward the surface and can finally make out the sky and sun above.

"Hello, Sonny," says a customer.

"Hello!" he replies. "Nice to see you. Can I help you with something?"

"I need four copies of *Mrs. Frisby and the Rats of NIMH*, by Robert O'Brien, and four copies of *The Saturdays*, by Elizabeth Enright."

"Four of each? That's a lot."

The customer nods. "I know."

"I think we have one or two of each," says Sonny, checking the computer, "but not four. Have you tried Cover to Cover? They might have more."

"I'll go there next."

Sonny directs the customer to the children's section of the store, taking great pleasure in this small task.

Now walk outside of town, far into the country surrounding Camden Falls. Turn onto the gravel drive and approach the plain house at the end, the one that looks careworn and cared for at the same time. It belongs to the Shermans, who have had a most momentous year. Mrs. Sherman isn't at home. She's on a job interview, and if she gets the job (which she isn't sure about at all), the Shermans' lives will become much more comfortable.

On this warm day, Nikki and her little sister, Mae, are in the dusty yard, throwing an old tennis ball for their dog, Paw-Paw.

"He's good about catching it but not very good about bringing it back," observes Mae.

"That's okay. He's having fun," says Nikki, and she throws the ball again. It lands in the bushes at the edge of their property, and Paw-Paw dashes to the bushes, then skids to a halt and looks helplessly at Nikki and Mae. Where did his ball go?

"I'll find it," says Mae.

Inside, their older brother, Tobias, has an hour before he needs to leave for one of his part-time jobs. He reaches for the TV remote, then withdraws his hand and heads for the kitchen instead. He sits down at the table, turns on the computer, and finds the Web site for the small college to which he has hastily and secretly applied.

Now walk back to town and turn onto Aiken Avenue. In the block just north of Dodds Lane are the Row Houses, where two small but momentous things are happening. Look first in the backyard of the second house from the left. There's Mr. Willet. He's sitting at his picnic table, leafing through a packet of materials from Three Oaks, where his wife now resides. He finds the pamphlet describing the apartments available for independent living and tries to imagine himself in a two-bedroom, which is what he would like. If he lived in one, he would be just minutes away from his wife.

Mr. Willet sighs. He removes his glasses and gazes around his yard. He can't believe he's thinking of leaving this place, his home for so many years. But he didn't realize how heart-wrenchingly difficult it would feel to be separated from Mary Lou, and he knows he can't live this way for much longer.

Four houses away, Mr. Pennington is lost in thought. He's standing in his living room, his hand resting on his trumpet case, and thinking that it might be time to ask Min Read out to dinner again, just the two of them. Would she like to go to Fig Tree? "What do you think, Jacques?" he asks the old cocker spaniel, and Jacques thumps his tail on the floor.

Now leave the Row Houses behind, take a stroll along shady streets, turn up a flagstone walk, and peek in another window. Someone is very busy at a desk in the study. This person, the one who was a customer at Time and Again an hour ago, has arranged four mailing envelopes on the desk, and placed one copy of *The Saturdays* and one copy of *Mrs. Frisby and the Rats of NIMH* on each envelope. On top of each stack of books a letter is now placed. The letter informs the recipient that these titles are the first selection in a secret summer book club, and that every few weeks until school starts again, another selection will arrive. The sender of the letter hopes the recipient will enjoy the books and the conversations and activities they spark. The sender does not sign any of the letters.

Come closer and take a good look in the study. The person at the desk is busy and won't notice you. Watch as each envelope is stuffed with the books and letter. Now watch as the person writes a name on each envelope: Flora, Ruby, Olivia, Nikki.

The person seated at the desk smiles and thinks about the Camden Falls summer that stretches ahead.

**Ann M. Martin**

*talks about*

Q: Who was your best friend growing up? What were some of the things you'd do together?

A: My best friend was Beth McKeever. We met when we were four years old — and we're still friends! When we were growing up, we lived on the same street, and we spent tons of time together. In fact, half of the entries in the diary my mother kept for me say that either Beth spent the night at our house or I spent the night at hers. We invented clubs, played outdoors with the other kids in the neighborhood, watched Soupy Sales and *The Mickey Mouse Club* on television, and put on plays with my sister. When we were older, we went to the Jersey Shore, went shopping, learned how to sew, took long bike rides, and spent plenty of time on the telephone.

Q: In this book, Flora has trouble when her old best friend and her new best friend don't get along (at first). Have you ever been in that situation? Any advice for someone who is?

A: I haven't been specifically in Flora's situation, but I do know that introducing two friends can be tricky. It can go well — or one or both friends can experience a bit of jealousy, as Olivia and Annika did. The important thing to remember is that your friends are jealous because they like *you* so much, and they want to be certain they'll remain your friends.

Assure each of them that you have room for plenty of friends in your life, and tell them you want your friends to get to know each other as well as they know you. Your friendships may expand, but you hope to remain best friends (with both of them) forever.

Q: A lot of readers have asked what Flora's life back in her old town, with Annika, was like. How do you think that town was different from Camden Falls?

A: Flora's old town was bigger than Camden Falls, and there was less of a sense of community. Flora comments at one point that she didn't know the shopkeepers in her old home, as she does the shopkeepers on Main Street. However, Flora still remembers her home fondly. After all, she grew up there. She had friends there and knew her neighbors. But she didn't feel as connected to the community as she does to the Row House families, to Main Street, and to Camden Falls.

**Q: What are some things you and your best friends do now?**

A: Some of my best friends no longer live nearby so we don't get to see each other as often as we used to. We keep in touch via e-mail and the telephone.

When we do get together, we like to go out to dinner, go shopping, or maybe take a trip. One of my best friends these days is my sister. We talk on the phone a lot, and I love spending time with her family. We've gone to Disney World twice, we go to the theatre (we love musicals), and we especially like to play board games and word games. I do different things with different friends. One of my favorite pastimes is simply hanging out at my house — reading or talking on the porch, watching videos or doing arts and crafts with my friends and their kids. We're never at a loss for something to do!

**Q: What's your favorite 'best friend' memory?**

A: I have so many memories from the years when Beth and I were neighbors that it's hard to choose one favorite, but we do have a lot of great Christmas memories. Every year on Christmas Eve day, we would get together and try to pass the long hours until Christmas Eve by making a large mural depicting a holiday scene. We drew the same scene year after year. I wonder where those murals are now.

# Spend some time on

## Main Street

**Welcome to Camden Falls** · **Needle and Thread** · **'Tis the Season**

# M[██████████] able stories
[██████████] Martin…

$W$hen their mother is
[ta]ken away from them,
[st]ray pups Squirrel and
[B]one are forced to ma[ke]
[it] on their own—bravi[ng]
[h]umans, busy highways[,]
[a]nd all kinds of weath[er.]

n M. Martin

[Cor]ner of the Universe

Newbe[ry]
Hono[r]
Book

turned her world
upside down.

**SCHOLASTIC**

www.scholastic.com/annmartin

SCHOLASTIC and associated logos are trademarks and/or registered trademarks of Scholastic Inc.

UN